HARD CANDY

D0094573

By TENNESSEE WILLIAMS

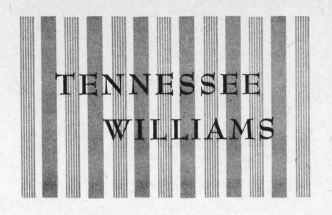

TENNESSEE
WILLIAMS

HARD
CANDY

A BOOK OF STORIES

A NEW DIRECTIONS BOOK

Library of Congress catalog card number:
59-16430

Note: The following stories included in this
collection were previously copyrighted as
follows:

Rubio y Morena, copyright 1948 by Tennessee Williams.

*The Resemblance Between a Violin Case
and a Coffin,* copyright 1950 by Tennessee Williams.

Three Players of a Summer Game, copyright
1952 by Tennessee Williams.

*The Coming of Something to the Widow
Holly,* copyright 1953 by Tennessee
Williams.

The Vine, copyright 1954 by Street & Smith,
Inc.

Acknowledgment is made to the editors of
*New Directions Annual, Flair, The New
Yorker,* and *Mademoiselle* in whose pages
certain of these stories were first printed.

First published as New Directions Paper-
book 225 in 1967. (ISBN: 0-8112-0221-6)

Manufactured in the United States of
America.

Published in Canada by
McClelland & Stewart, Ltd.

New Directions Books are published
for James Laughlin by
New Directions Publishing Corporation,
333 Sixth Avenue, New York 10014.

FIFTH PRINTING

FOR —
JANE AND PAUL BOWLES

impalpable
lambency

EDITOR'S NOTE

Two of the stories in this volume, *Hard Candy* and *Mysteries of the Joy Rio*, are variations on the same theme and employ the same setting; they are so different in result that it was thought both would be of interest. *Hard Candy* is the later version.

CONTENTS

THREE PLAYERS OF
A SUMMER GAME

THREE PLAYERS
OF A
SUMMER GAME

CROQUET is a summer game that seems, in a curious way, to be composed of images the way that a painter's abstraction of summer or one of its games would be built of them. The delicate wire wickets set in a lawn of smooth emerald that flickers fierily at some points and rests under violet shadow in others, the wooden poles gaudily painted as moments that stand out in a season that was a struggle for something of unspeakable importance to someone passing through it, the clean and hard wooden spheres of different colors and the strong rigid shape of the mallets that drive the balls through the wickets, the formal design of those wickets and poles upon the croquet lawn — all of these are like a painter's abstraction of a summer and a game played in it. And

9

I cannot think of croquet without hearing a sound like the faraway boom of a cannon fired to announce a white ship coming into a harbor which had expected it anxiously for a long while. The faraway booming sound is that of a green-and-white striped awning coming down over a gallery of a white frame house. The house is of Victorian design carried to an extreme of improvisation, an almost grotesque pile of galleries and turrets and cupolas and eaves, all freshly painted white, so white and so fresh that it has the blue-white glitter of a block of ice in the sun. The house is like a new resolution not yet tainted by any defection from it. And I associate the summer game with players coming out of this house, out of the mysteries of a walled place, with the buoyant air of persons just released from a suffocating enclosure, as if they had spent the fierce day bound in a closet, were breathing freely at last in fresh atmosphere and able to move without hindrance. Their clothes are as light in weight and color as the flattering clothes of dancers. There are three players — a woman, a man, and a child.

The voice of the woman player is not at all a loud one; yet it has a pleasantly resonant quality that carries it farther than most voices go and it is interspersed with peals of treble laughter, pitched much higher than the voice itself, which are cool-sounding as particles of ice in a tall shaken glass. This woman player, even more than her male opponent in the game, has the grateful quickness of motion of someone let out of a suffocating enclosure; her motion has the quickness of breath released just after a moment of terror, of fingers unclenched when panic is suddenly past or of a cry that subsides into laughter. She seems unable to speak or move about moderately; she moves in convulsive rushes, whipping her skirts with long strides that quicken to running. The whipped skirts are white ones. They make a faint crackling sound as her pumping thighs whip them open, the sound that comes to you, greatly diminished by distance, when fitful fair-weather gusts belly out and slacken the faraway sails of a yawl. That agreeably cool summer sound is accompanied by another which is even cooler, the ceaseless tiny chatter of beads hung in long loops from her throat. They are not pearls but they have a milky luster, they are small faintly speckled white ovals, polished bird's eggs turned solid and strung upon glittery filaments of silver. This woman player is never still for a moment; sometimes she exhausts herself and collapses on the grass in the conscious attitudes of a dancer. She is a thin woman with long bones and skin of a silky luster and her eyes are only a shade or two darker than the blue-tinted bird's-egg beads about her long throat. She is never still, not even when she has fallen in exhaustion on the grass. The neighbors think she's gone mad but they feel no pity for her, and that, of course, is because of her male opponent in the game.

This player is Brick Pollitt, a man so tall with such a fiery thatch of hair on top of him that I never see a flagpole on an expanse of green lawn or even a particularly brilliant cross or weather vane on a steeple without thinking suddenly of that long-ago summer and Brick Pollitt and begin to assort again the baffling bits and pieces that make his legend. These bits and pieces, these assorted images, they are like the paraphernalia for a game of croquet, gathered up from the lawn when the game is over and packed carefully into an oblong wooden box which they just exactly fit and fill. There they all are, the bits and pieces, the images, the apparently incongruous paraphernalia of a summer that was the last one of my childhood, and now I take them out of the oblong box and arrange them once more in the formal design on the lawn. It would be absurd to pretend that this is altogether the way it was, and yet it may be closer than a literal history could be to the hidden truth of it. Brick Pollitt is the male player of this summer game, and he is a drinker who has not yet completely fallen beneath the savage axe blows of his liquor. He is not so young any more but he has not yet lost the slim grace of his youth. He is a head taller than the tall woman player of the game. He is such a tall man that, even in those sections of the lawn dimmed under violet shadow, his head continues to catch fiery rays of the descending sun, the way that the heavenward pointing index finger of that huge gilded hand atop a Protestant steeple in Meridian goes on drawing the sun's flame for a good while after the lower surfaces of the town have sunk into lingering dusk.

The third player of the summer game is the daughter of the woman, a plump twelve-year-old child named Mary Louise. This little girl had made herself distinctly unpopular among the children of the neighborhood by imitating too perfectly the elegant manners and cultivated eastern voice of her mother. She sat in the electric automobile on the sort of a fat silk pillow that expensive lap dogs sit on, uttering treble peals of ladylike laughter,

12

tossing her curls, using grown-up expressions such as, "Oh, how delightful" and "Isn't that just lovely." She would sit in the electric automobile sometimes all afternoon by herself as if she were on display in a glass box, only now and then raising a plaintive voice to call her mother and ask if it was all right for her to come in now or if she could drive the electric around the block, which she was sometimes then permitted to do.

I was her only close friend and she was mine. Sometimes she called me over to play croquet with her but that was only when her mother and Brick Pollitt had disappeared into the house too early to play the game. Mary Louise had a passion for croquet; she played it for itself, without any more shadowy and important connotations.

What the game meant to Brick Pollitt calls for some further account of Brick's life before that summer. He was a young Delta planter who had been a celebrated athlete at Sewanee, who had married a New Orleans debutante who was a Mardi Gras queen and whose father owned a fleet of banana boats. It had seemed a brilliant marriage, with lots of wealth and prestige on both sides, but only two years later Brick had started falling in love with his liquor and Margaret, his wife, began to be praised for her patience and loyalty to him. Brick seemed to be throwing his life away as if it were something disgusting that he had suddenly found in his hands. This self-disgust came upon him with the abruptness and violence of a crash on a highway. But what had Brick crashed into? Nothing that anybody was able to surmise, for he seemed to have everything that young men like Brick might hope or desire to have. What else is there? There must have been something else that he wanted and lacked, or what reason was there for dropping his life and taking hold of a glass which he never let go of for more than one waking hour? His wife, Margaret, took hold of Brick's ten-thousand-acre plantation as firmly and surely as if she had always existed for that and no other purpose. She had Brick's power of attorney and she managed all of his business affairs with celebrated astuteness. "He'll come out of it," she said. "Brick is passing through something that he'll come out of." She always said the right thing; she took the conventionally right attitude and expressed it to the world that admired her for it. She had never committed any apostasy from the social faith she was born to and everybody admired her as a remarkably fine and brave little woman who had too much to put up with. Two sections of an hourglass could not drain and fill more evenly than Brick and Margaret changed places after he took to drink. It was as though she had her lips fastened to some invisible wound in his body through which drained out of him and flowed into her the assurance and vitality that he had owned before marriage. Margaret Pollitt lost her pale, feminine prettiness and assumed in its place something more impressive — a firm and rough-textured sort of handsomeness that came out of her indefinite chrysalis as mysteriously as one of those metamorphoses that occur in insect life. Once very pretty but indistinct, a graceful sketch that was done with a very light pencil, she became vivid as Brick disappeared behind the veil of his liquor. She came out of a mist. She rose into clarity as Brick descended. She abruptly stopped being quiet and dainty. She was now apt to have dirty fingernails which she covered with scarlet enamel. When the enamel chipped off, the gray showed underneath. Her hair was now cut short so that she didn't have to "mess with it." It was wind-blown and full of sparkle; she jerked a comb through it to make it crackle. She had white teeth that were a little too large for her thin lips, and when she threw her head back in laughter, strong cords of muscle stood out in her smooth brown throat. She had a booming laugh that she might have stolen from Brick while he was drunk or asleep beside her at night. She had a practice of releasing the clutch on a car and shooting off in high gear at the exact instant that her laughter boomed out, not calling goodbye but thrusting out one bare strong arm, straight out as a piston with fingers clenched into a fist, as the car whipped up and disappeared into a cloud of yellow dust. She didn't drive her own little runabout nowadays so much as she did Brick's Pierce-Arrow touring car, for Brick's driver's license had been revoked. She frequently broke the speed limit on the highway. The patrolmen would stop her, but she had such an affability, such a disarming way with her, that they would have a good laugh together, she and the highway patrolman, and he would tear up the ticket.

Somebody in her family died in Memphis that spring, and she went there to attend the funeral and collect her inheritance, and while she was gone on that profitable journey, Brick Pollitt slipped out from under her thumb a bit. Another death occurred during her absence. That

nice young doctor who took care of Brick when he had
to be carried to the hospital, he suddenly took sick in a
shocking way. An awful flower grew in his brain like a
fierce geranium that shattered its pot. All of a sudden
the wrong words came out of his mouth; he seemed to
be speaking in an unknown tongue; he couldn't find
things with his hands; he made troubled signs over his
forehead. His wife led him about the house by one hand,
yet he stumbled and fell flat; the breath was knocked
out of him, and he had to be put to bed by his wife and
the Negro yardman; and he lay there laughing weakly,
incredulously, trying to find his wife's hand with both
of his while she looked at him with eyes that she couldn't
keep from blazing with terror. He stayed under drugs
for a week, and it was during that time that Brick Pollitt
came to see her. Brick came and sat with Isabel Grey by
her dying husband's bed and she couldn't speak, she
could only shake her head, incessantly as a metronome,
with no lips visible in her white face, but two pressed
narrow bands of a dimmer whiteness that shook as if
some white liquid flowed beneath them with an incred-
ible rapidity and violence which made them quiver . . .

God was the only word she was able to say; but Brick
Pollitt somehow understood what she meant by that
word, as if it were in a language that she and he, alone
of all people, could speak and understand; and when
the dying man's eyes forcibly opened on something they
couldn't bear to look at, it was Brick, his hands suddenly
quite sure and steady, who filled the hypodermic needle
for her and pumped its contents fiercely into her husband's hard young arm. And it was over. There was

16

another bed at the back of the house and he and Isabel lay beside each other on that bed for a couple of hours before they let the town know that her hubsand's agony was completed, and the only movement between them was the intermittent, spasmodic digging of their fingernails into each other's clenched palm while their bodies lay stiffly separate, deliberately not touching at any other points as if they abhorred any other contact with each other, while this intolerable thing was ringing like an iron bell through them.

And so you see what the summer game on the violet-shadowed lawn was — it was a running together out of something unbearably hot and bright into something obscure and cool ...

THE young widow was left with nothing in the way of material possessions except the house and an electric automobile, but by the time Brick's wife, Margaret, had returned from her profitable journey to Memphis, Brick had taken over the post-catastrophic details of the widow's life. For a week or two, people thought it was very kind of him, and then all at once public opinion changed and they decided that Brick's reason for kindness was by no means noble. It appeared to observers that the widow was now his mistress, and this was true. It was true in the limited way that most such opinions are true. It is only the outside of one person's world that is visible to others, and all opinions are false ones, especially public opinions of individual cases. She was his mistress, but that was not Brick's reason. His reason had something to do with that chaste interlocking of hands their first time together, after the hypodermic; it had to do with those hours, now receding and fading behind them as all such hours must, but neither of them could have said what it was aside from that. Neither of them was able to think very clearly about the matter. But Brick was able to pull himself together for a while and take command of those post-catastrophic details in the young widow's life and her daughter's.

The daughter, Mary Louise, was a plump child of twelve. She was my friend that summer. Mary Louise and I caught lightning bugs and put them in Mason jars to make flickering lanterns, and we played the game of croquet when her mother and Brick Pollitt were not inclined to play it. It was Mary Louise that summer who taught me how to deal with mosquito bites. She was plagued by mosquitoes and so was I. She warned me that scratching the bites would leave scars on my skin, which was as tender as hers. I said that I didn't care. "Someday you will," she told me. She carried with her constantly that summer a lump of ice in a handkerchief. Whenever a mosquito bit her, instead of scratching the bite she rubbed it gently with the handkerchief-wrapped lump of ice until the sting was frozen to numbness. Of course, in five minutes it would come back and have to be frozen again, but eventually it would disappear and leave no scar. Mary Louise's skin, where it was not temporarily mutilated by a mosquito bite or a slight rash that sometimes appeared after eating strawberry ice cream, was ravishingly smooth and tender. The association is not at all a proper one, but how can you recall a summer in childhood without some touches of impropriety? I can't remember Mary Louise's plump bare legs and arms, fragrant with sweet-pea powder, without also thinking of an afternoon drive we took in the electric automobile to the little art museum that had recently been established in the town. We went there just before the five o'clock closing time, and straight as a bee, Mary Louise led me into a room that was devoted to replicas of famous antique sculptures. There was a reclining male nude (the "Dying Gaul," I believe) and it was straight to this statue that she led me. I began to blush before we arrived there. It was naked except for a fig leaf, which was of a different-colored metal from the bronze of the prostrate figure, and to my astonished horror, that afternoon, Mary Louise, after a quick, sly look in all directions, picked the fig leaf up, removed it from what it covered, and then turned her totally un-embarrassed and innocent eyes upon mine and inquired, smiling very brightly, "Is yours like that?"

My answer was idiotic; I said, "I don't know!" and I think I was blushing long after we left the museum ...

The Greys' house in the spring when the doctor died of brain cancer was very run down. But soon after Brick Pollitt started coming over to see the young widow, the house was painted; it was painted so white that it was almost a very pale blue; it had the blue-white glitter of a block of ice in the sun. Coolness of appearance seemed to be the most desired of all things that summer. In spite of his red hair, Brick Pollitt had a cool appearance be-cause he was still young and thin, as thin as the widow, and he dressed as she did in clothes of light weight and color. His white shirts looked faintly pink because of his

skin underneath them. Once, I saw him through an upstairs window of the widow's house just a moment before
he pulled the shade down. I was in an upstairs room of my
house and I saw that Brick Pollitt was divided into two
colors as distinct as two stripes of a flag, the upper part of
him, which had been exposed to the sun, almost crimson
and the lower part of him white as this piece of paper.

While the widow's house was being repainted (at
Brick Pollitt's expense), she and her daughter lived at
the Alcazar Hotel, also at Brick's expense. Brick super-
vised the renovation of the widow's house. He drove in
from his plantation every morning to watch the house
painters and gardeners at work. Brick's driving license
had been restored to him, and it was an important step
forward in his personal renovation—being able to drive
his own car again. He drove it with elaborate caution
and formality, coming to a dead stop at every cross street
in the town, sounding the silver trumpet at every corner,
inviting pedestrians to precede him, with smiles and
bows and great circular gestures of his hands. But observers did not approve of what Brick Pollitt was doing.
They sympathized with his wife, Margaret, that brave
little woman who had to put up with so much. As for
Dr. Grey's widow, she had not been very long in the
town; the doctor had married her while he was an in-
terne at a big hospital in Baltimore. Nobody had formed
a definite opinion of her before the doctor died, so it was
no effort, now, to simply condemn her, without any
qualification, as a strumpet, common in everything but
her "affectations."

Brick Pollitt, when he talked to the house painters,

shouted to them as if they were deaf, so that all the neighbors could hear what he had to say. He was explaining things to the world, especially the matter of his drinking.

"It's something," he shouted, "that you can't cut out completely right away. That's the big mistake that most drinkers make — they try to cut it out completely, and you can't do that. You can do it for maybe a month or two months, but all at once you go back on it worse than before you went off it, and then the discouragement is awful — you lose all faith in yourself and just give up. The thing to do, the way to handle the problem, is like a bullfighter handles a bull in a ring. Wear it down little by little, get control of it gradually. That's how I'm handling this thing! Yep. Now, let's say that you get up wanting a drink in the morning. Say it's ten o'clock, maybe. Well, you say to yourself, 'Just wait half an hour, old boy, and then you can have one.' Well, at half-past ten you still want that drink, and you want it a little bit worse than you did at ten, but you say to yourself, 'Boy, you could do without it half an hour ago so you can do without it now.' You see, that's how you got to argue about it with yourself, because a drinking man is not one person — a man that drinks is two people, one grabbing the bottle, the other one fighting him off it, not one but two people fighting each other to get control of a bottle. Well, sir, if you can talk yourself out of a drink at ten, you can still talk yourself out of a drink at *half-past* ten! But at *eleven* o'clock the need for the drink is greater. Now *here's* the important thing to remember about this struggle. You got to watch those scales, and when they tip too far against your power to resist, you got to give in a little. That's not weakness. *That's strategy!* Because don't forget what I told you. A drinking man is not one person but two, and it's a battle of wits going on between them. And so I say at eleven, 'Well, *have* your drink at that hour, *go on*, and *have* it! One drink at eleven won't hurt you!'

"What time is it, now? Yep! Eleven . . . All right, I'm going to have me that one drink. I could do without it, I don't crave it, but the important thing is . . ."

His voice would trail off as he entered the widow's house. He would stay in there longer than it took to have one drink, and when he came out, there was a change in his voice as definite as a change of weather or season, the strong and vigorous tone would be a bit filmed over.

Then he would usually talk about his wife. "I don't say my wife Margaret's not an intelligent woman. She is, and both of us know it, but she don't have a good head for property values. Now, you know Dr. Grey, who used to live here before that brain thing killed him. Well, he was my physician, he pulled me through some bad times when I had that liquor problem. I felt I owed him a lot. Now, that was a terrible thing the way he went, but it was terrible for his widow, too; she was left with this house and that electric automobile and that's all, and this house was put up for sale to pay off her debts, and — well, I bought it. I bought it, and now I'm giving it back to her. Now, my wife Margaret, she. And a lot of other folks, too. Don't understand about this . . .

"What time is it? Twelve? High noon! . . . This ice is melted . . ."

22

He'd drift back into the house and stay there half an hour, and when he came back out, it was rather shyly with a sad and uncertain creaking of the screen door pushed by the hand not holding the tall glass, but after resting a little while on the steps, he would resume his talk to the house painters.

"Yes," he would say, as if he had only paused a moment before, "it's the most precious thing that a woman can give to a man — his lost respect for himself — and the meanest thing one human being can do to another human being is take his respect for himself away from him. I. I had it took away from me . . ."

The glass would tilt slowly up and jerkily down, and he'd have to wipe his chin dry.

"I had it took away from me! I won't tell you how, but maybe, being men about my age, you're able to guess it. That was how. Some of them don't want it. They cut it off. They cut it right off a man, and half the time he don't even know when they cut it off him. Well, I knew it all right. I could feel it being cut off me. Do you know what I mean? . . . That's right . . .

"But once in a while there's one — and they don't come often — that wants for a man to keep it, and those are the women that God made and put on this earth. The other kind come out of hell, or out of . . . I don't know what. I'm talking too much. Sure. I know I'm talking too much about private matters. But that's all right. This property is mine. I'm talking on my own property and I don't give a s—— who hears me! I'm not shouting about it, but I'm not sneaking around about it neither. Whatever I do, I do it without any shame,

23

and I've got a right to do it. I've been through a hell of
a lot that nobody knows. But I'm coming out of it now.
God damn it, yes, I am! I can't take all the credit. And
yet I'm proud. I'm goddam proud of myself, because I
was in a pitiful condition with that liquor problem of
mine, but now the worst is over. I've got it just about
licked. That's my car out there and I drove it up here
myself. It's no short drive, it's almost a hundred miles,
and I drive it each morning and drive it back each night.
I've got back my driver's license, and I fired the man
that was working for my wife, looking after our place.
I fired that man and not only fired him but give him a
kick in the britches that'll make him eat standing up for
the next week or two. It wasn't because I thought he was
fooling around. It wasn't that. But him and her both
took about the same attitude toward me, and I didn't
like the attitude they took. They would talk about me
right in front of me, as if I wasn't there. 'Is it time for
his medicine?' Yes, they were giving me dope! So one
day I played possum. I was lying out there on the sofa
and she said to him, 'I guess he's passed out now.' And
he said, 'Jesus, dead drunk at half-past one in the afternoon!' Well. I got up slowly. I wasn't drunk at that
hour, I wasn't even half drunk. I stood up straight and
walked slowly toward him. I walked straight up to
them both, and you should of seen the eyes of them
both bug out! 'Yes, Jesus,' I said, 'at half-past one!' And
I grabbed him by his collar and by the seat of his britches
and turkey-trotted him right on out of the house and
pitched him on his face in a big mud puddle at the foot
of the steps to the front verandah. And as far as I know or

24

care, maybe he's still laying there and she's still scream-
ing, 'Stop, Brick!' But I believe I did hit her. Yes, I did.
I did hit her. There's times when you got to hit them,
and that was one of those times. I ain't been to the house
since. I moved in the little place we lived in before the
big one was built, on the other side of the bayou, and
ain't crossed over there since . . .

"Well, sir, that's all over with now. I got back my
power of attorney which I'd give to that woman and I
got back my driver's license and I bought this piece of
property in town and signed my own check for it and
I'm having it completely done over to make it as handsome a piece of residential property as you can find in
this town, and I'm having that lawn out there prepared
for the game of croquet."

Then he'd look at the glass in his hands as if he had
just then noticed that he was holding it; he'd give it a
look of slightly pained surprise, as if he had cut his hand
and just now noticed that it was cut and bleeding. Then
he would sigh like an old-time actor in a tragic role. He
would put the tall glass down on the balustrade with
great, great care, look back at it to make sure that it
wasn't going to fall over, and walk very straight and
steady to the porch steps and just as steady but with
more concentration down them. When he arrived at the
foot of the steps, he would laugh as if someone had made
a comical remark; he would duck his head genially and
shout to the house painters something like this: "Well,
I'm not making any predictions because I'm no fortune-
teller, but I've got a strong idea that I'm going to lick
my liquor problem this summer, ha ha, I'm going to lick

it this summer! I'm not going to take no cure and I'm not going to take no pledge, I'm just going to prove I'm a man with his balls back on him! I'm going to do it step by little step, the way that people play the game of croquet. You know how you play that game. You hit the ball through one wicket and then you drive it through the next one. You hit it through that wicket and then you drive on to another. You go from wicket to wicket, and it's a game of precision — it's a game that takes concentration and precision, and that's what makes it a wonderful game for a drinker. It takes a sober man to play a game of precision. It's better than shooting pool, because a pool hall is always next door to a gin mill, and you never see a pool player that don't have his liquor glass on the edge of the table or somewhere pretty near it, and croquet is also a better game than golf, because in golf you've always got that nineteenth hole waiting for you. Nope, for a man with a liquor problem, croquet is a summer game and it may seem a little bit sissy, but let me tell you, it's a game of precision. You go from wicket to wicket until you arrive at that big final pole, and then, bang, you've hit it, the game is finished, you're there! And then, and not until then, you can go up here to the porch and have you a cool gin drink, a buck or a Collins — Hey! Where did I leave that glass? Aw! Yeah, hand it down to me, will you? Ha ha — thanks."

He would take a birdlike sip, make a fiercely wry face, and shake his head violently as if somebody had drenched it with scalding water.

"This God damn stuff!" He would look around to find a safe place to set the glass down again. He would

26

select a bare spot of earth between the hydrangea bushes, deposit the glass there as carefully as if he were planting a memorial tree, and then he would straighten up with a great air of relief and expand his chest and flex his arms. "Ha, ha, yep, croquet is a summer game for widows and drinkers, ha ha!"

For a few moments, standing there in the sun, he would seem as sure and powerful as the sun itself; but then some little shadow of uncertainty would touch him again, get through the wall of his liquor, some tricky little shadow of a thought, as sly as a mouse, quick, dark, too sly to be caught, and without his moving enough for it to be noticed, his still fine body would fall as violently as a giant tree crashes down beneath a final axe stroke, taking with it all the wheeling seasons of sun and stars, whole centuries of them, crashing suddenly into oblivion and rot. He would make this enormous fall without a perceptible movement of his body. At the most, it would show in the faint flicker of something across his face, whose color gave him the name people knew him by. Something flickered across his flame-colored face. Possibly one knee sagged a little forward. Then slowly, slowly, the way a bull trots uncertainly back from its first wild, challenging plunge into the ring, he would fasten one hand over his belt and raise the other one hesitantly to his head, feeling the scalp and the hard round bowl of the skull underneath it, as if he dimly imagined that by feeling that dome he might be able to guess what was hidden inside it, the dark and wondering stuff beneath that dome of calcium, facing, now, the intricate wickets of the summer to come . . .

For one reason or another, Mary Louise Grey was locked out of the house a great deal of the time that summer, and since she was a lonely child with little or no imagination, apparently unable to amuse herself with solitary games — except the endless one of copying her mother — the afternoons that she was excluded from the house "because Mother has a headache" were periods of great affliction. There were several galleries with outside stairs between them, and she patrolled the galleries and wandered forlornly about the lawn, and from time to time, she went down the front walk and sat in the glass box of the electric. She would vary her steps, sometimes walking sedately, sometimes skipping, sometimes hopping and humming, one plump hand always clutching the handkerchief that contained the lump of ice. This lump of ice to rub her mosquito bites had to be replaced at frequent intervals. "Oh, iceman," the widow would call sweetly from an upstairs window, "don't forget to leave some extra pieces for little Mary Louise to rub her mosquito bites with!"

Each time a new bite was suffered Mary Louise would utter a soft cry in a voice that had her mother's trick of carrying a great distance without being loud.

"Oh, Mother," she would moan, "I'm simply being devoured by mosquitoes!"

"Darling," her mother would answer, "that's dreadful, but you know that Mother can't help it; she didn't create the mosquitoes and she can't destroy them for you!"

"You could let me come in the house, Mama."

"No, I can't let you come in, precious. Not yet."

"Why not, Mother?"'

"Because Mother has a sick headache."

"I will be quiet."

"You say that you will, but you won't. You must learn to amuse yourself, precious; you mustn't depend on Mother to amuse you. Nobody can depend on anyone else forever. I'll tell you what you can do till Mother's headache is better. You can drive the electric out of the garage. You can drive it around the block, but don't go into the business district with it, and then you can stop in the shady part of the drive and sit there perfectly comfortably till Mother feels better and can get dressed and come out. And then I think Mr. Pollitt may come over for a game of crocquet. Won't that be lovely?"

"Do you think he will get here in time to play?"

"I hope so, precious. It does him so much good to play croquet."

"Oh, I think it does all of us good to play croquet," said Mary Louise in a voice that trembled just at the vision of it.

Before Brick Pollitt arrived — sometimes half an hour before his coming, as though she could hear his automobile on the highway thirty miles from the house — Mary Louise would bound plumply off the gallery and begin setting up the poles and wickets of the longed-for game. While she was doing this, her plump little buttocks and her beginning breasts and her shoulder-length copper curls would all bob up and down in perfect unison.

I would watch her from the steps of my house on the diagonally opposite corner of the street. She worked feverishly against time, for experience had taught her the sooner she completed the preparations for the game the greater would be the chance of getting her mother and Mr. Pollitt to play it. Frequently she was not fast enough, or they were too fast for her. By the time she had finished her perspiring job, the verandah was often deserted. Her wailing cries would begin, punctuating the dusk at intervals only a little less frequent than the passing of cars of people going out for evening drives to cool off.

"Mama! Mama! The croquet set is ready!"

Usually there would be a long, long wait for any response to come from the upstairs window toward which the calls were directed. But one time there wasn't. Almost immediately after the wailing voice was lifted, begging for the commencement of the game, Mary Louise's thin pretty mother showed herself at the window. She came to the window like a white bird flying into some unnoticed obstruction. That was the time when I saw, between the dividing gauze of the bedroom curtains, her naked breasts, small and beautiful, shaken like two angry fists by her violent motion. She leaned between the curtains to answer Mary Louise not in her usual tone of gentle remonstrance but in a shocking cry of rage: "Oh, be still, for God's sake, you fat little monster!"

Mary Louise was shocked into petrified silence that must have lasted for a quarter of an hour. It was probably the word "fat" that struck her so overwhelmingly, for Mary Louise had once told me, when we were circling the block in the electric, that her mother had told her that she was *not* fat, that she was only plump, and that these cushions of flesh were going to dissolve in two or three more years and then she would be just as thin and pretty as her mother.

Sometimes Mary Louise would call me over to play croquet with her, but she was not at all satisfied with my game. I had had so little practice and she so much, and besides, more importantly, it was the company of the grown-up people she wanted. She would call me over only when they had disappeared irretrievably into the lightless house or when the game had collapsed owing to Mr. Brick Pollitt's refusal to take it seriously. When he played seriously, he was even better at it than Mary Louise, who practiced her strokes sometimes all afternoon in preparation for a game. But there were evenings when he would not leave his drink on the porch but would carry it down onto the lawn with him and would play with one hand, more and more capriciously, while in the other hand he carried the tall glass. Then the lawn would become a great stage on which he performed all the immemorial antics of the clown, to the exasperation of Mary Louise and her thin, pretty mother, both of whom would become very severe and dignified on these occasions. They would retire from the croquet lawn and stand off at a little distance, calling softly, "Brick, Brick" and "Mr. Pollitt," like a pair of complaining doves, both in the same ladylike tones of remonstrance. He was not a middle-aged-looking man — that is, he was not at all big around the middle — and he could leap and run like a boy. He could turn cartwheels and walk on his hands, and sometimes he would grunt and lunge like a wrestler or make long crouching runs like a football player, weaving in and out among the wickets and gaudily painted poles of the croquet lawn. The acrobatics and sports of his youth seemed to haunt him. He called out hoarsely to invisible teammates and adversaries — muffled shouts of defiance and anger and triumph, to which an incongruous counterpoint was continually provided by the faint, cooing voice of the widow, "Brick, Brick, stop now, please stop. The child is crying. People will think you've gone crazy." For Mary Louise's mother, despite the extreme ambiguity of her station in life, was a woman with a keener than ordinary sense of propriety. She knew why the lights had gone out on all the screened summer porches and why the automobiles drove past the house at the speed of a funeral procession while Mr. Brick Pollitt was making a circus ring of the croquet lawn.

Late one evening when he was making one of his crazy dashes across the lawn with an imaginary football hugged against his belly, he tripped over a wicket and sprawled on the lawn, and he pretended to be too gravely injured to get back on his feet. His loud groans brought Mary Louise and her mother running from behind the vine-screened end of the verandah and out upon the lawn to assist him. They took him by each hand and tried to haul him up, but with a sudden shout of laughter he pulled them both down on top of him and held them there till both of them were sobbing. He got up, finally, that evening, but it was only to replenish his glass of iced gin, and then returned to the lawn. That evening was a fearfully hot one, and Brick decided to cool and refresh himself with the sprinkler hose while he enjoyed his drink. He turned it on and pulled it out to the center of the lawn. There he rolled about the grass under its leisurely revolving arch of water, and as he rolled about, he began to wriggle out of his clothes. He kicked off his white shoes and one of his pale-green socks, tore off his drenched white shirt and grass-stained linen pants, but he never succeeded in getting off his necktie. Finally, he was sprawled, like some grotesque fountain figure, in underwear and necktie and the one remaining pale-green sock, while the revolving arch of water moved with cool whispers about him. The arch of water had a faint crystalline iridescence, a mist of delicate colors, as it wheeled under the moon, for the moon had by that time begun to poke with an air of slow astonishment over the roof of the little building that housed the electric. And still the complaining doves of the widow and her daughter cooed at him from various windows of the house, and you could tell their voices apart only by the fact that the mother murmured "Brick, Brick" and Mary Louise still called him Mr. Pollitt. "Oh, Mr. Pollitt, Mother is so unhappy, Mother is crying!"

That night he talked to himself or to invisible figures on the lawn. One of them was his wife, Margaret. He kept saying, "I'm sorry, Margaret, I'm sorry, Margaret, I'm so sorry, so sorry, Margaret. I'm sorry I'm no good, I'm sorry, Margaret, I'm so sorry, so sorry I'm no good, sorry I'm drunk, sorry I'm no good, I'm so sorry it all had to turn out like this . . ."

Later on, much later, after the remarkably slow procession of touring cars stopped passing the house, a little black sedan that belonged to the police came rushing up to the front walk and sat there for a while. In it was the chief of police himself. He called "Brick, Brick," almost as gently and softly as Mary Louise's mother had called him from the lightless windows. "Brick, Brick, old boy. Brick, fellow," till finally the inert fountain figure in underwear and green sock and unremovable necktie staggered out from under the rotating arch of water and stumbled down to the walk and stood there negligently and quietly conversing with the chief of police under the no longer at all astonished, now quite large and indifferent great yellow stare of the August moon. They began to laugh softly together, Mr. Brick Pollitt and the chief of police, and finally the door of the little black car opened and Mr. Brick Pollitt got in beside the chief of police while the common officer got out to collect the clothes, flabby as drenched towels, on the croquet lawn. Then they drove away, and the summer night's show was over . . .

It was not quite over for me, for I had been watching it all that time with unabated interest. And about an hour after the little black car of the very polite officers had driven away, I saw the mother of Mary Louise come out into the lawn; she stood there with an air of desolation for quite a while. Then she went into the small building in back of the house and drove out the electric. The electric went sedately out into the summer night, with its buzzing no louder than a summer insect's, and perhaps an hour later, for this was a very long night, it came back again containing in its glass show box not only the young and thin and pretty widow but a quiet and chastened Mr. Pollitt. She curved an arm about his immensely tall figure as they went up the front walk, and I heard him say only one word distinctly. It was the name of his wife.

Early that autumn, which was different from summer in nothing except the quicker coming of dusk, the visits of Mr. Brick Pollitt began to have the spasmodic irregularity of a stricken heart muscle. That faraway boom of a cannon at five o'clock was now the announcement that two ladies in white dresses were waiting on a white gallery for someone who was each time a little more likely to disappoint them than the time before. But disappointment was not a thing that Mary Louise was inured to; it was a country that she was passing through not as an old inhabitant but as a bewildered explorer, and each afternoon she removed the oblong yellow wood box, lugged it out of the little building in which it lived with the electric, ceremoniously opened it upon the center of the silken green lawn, and began to arrange the wickets in their formal pattern between the two gaudily painted poles that meant beginning, middle and end. And the widow, her mother, talked to her from the gallery, under the awning, as if there had been no important alteration in their lives or their prospects. Their almost duplicate voices as they talked back and forth between gallery and lawn rang out as clearly as if the enormous corner lot were enclosed at this hour by a still more enormous and perfectly translucent glass bell which picked up and carried through space what-

ever was uttered beneath it, and this was true not only
when they were talking across the lawn but when they
were seated side by side in the white wicker chairs on the
gallery. Phrases from these conversations became catch-
words, repeated and mocked by the neighbors, for whom
the widow and her daughter and Mr. Brick Pollitt had
been three players in a sensational drama which had
shocked and angered them for two acts but which now,
as it approached a conclusion, was declining into unin-
tentional farce, which they could laugh at. It was not difficult to find something ludicrous in the talks between
the two ladies or the high-pitched elegance of their voices.

Mary Louise would ask, "Will Mr. Pollitt get here in
time for croquet?"

"I hope so, precious. It does him so much good."

"He'll have to come soon or it will be too dark to see
the wickets."

"That's true, precious."

"Mother, why is it dark so early now?"

"Honey, you know why. The sun goes south."

"But why does it go south?"

"Precious, Mother cannot explain the movements of
the heavenly bodies, you know that as well as Mother
knows it. Those things are controlled by certain mysterious laws that people on earth don't know or understand."

"Mother, are we going east?"

"When, precious?"

"Before school starts."

"Honey, you know it's impossible for Mother to make
any definite plans."

"I hope we do. I don't want to go to school here."

"Why not, precious? Are you afraid of the children?"

"No, Mother, but they don't like me, they make fun of me."

"How do they make fun of you?"

"They mimic the way I talk and they walk in front of me with their stomachs pushed out and giggle."

"That's because they're children and children are cruel."

"Will they stop being cruel when they grow up?"

"Why, I suppose some of them will and some of them won't."

"Well, I hope we go east before school opens."

"Mother can't make any plans or promises, honey."

"No, but Mr. Brick Pollitt —"

"Honey, lower your voice! Ladies talk softly."

"Oh, my goodness!"

"What is it, precious?"

"A mosquito just bit me!"

"That's too bad, but don't scratch it. Scratching can leave a permanent scar on the skin."

"I'm not scratching it. I'm just sucking it, Mother."

"Honey, Mother has told you time and again that the thing to do when you have a mosquito bite is to get a small piece of ice and wrap it up in a handkerchief and rub the bite gently with it until the sting is removed."

"That's what I do, but my lump of ice is melted!"

"Get you another piece, honey. You know where the icebox is!"

"There's not much left. You put so much in the ice bag for your headache."

"There must be some left, honey."

"There's just enough left for Mr. Pollitt's drinks."

"Never mind that . . ."

"He needs it for his drinks, Mother."

"Yes, Mother knows what he wants the ice for, precious."

"There's only a little piece left. It's hardly enough to rub a mosquito bite with."

"Well, use it for that purpose, that purpose is better, and anyhow when Mr. Pollitt comes over as late as this, he doesn't deserve to have any ice saved for him."

"Mother?"

"Yes, precious?"

"I love ice and sugar!"

"What did you say, precious?"

"I said I loved ice and sugar!"

"Ice and sugar, precious?"

"Yes, I love the ice and sugar in the bottom of Mr. Pollitt's glass when he's through with it."

"Honey, you mustn't eat the ice in the bottom of Mr. Pollitt's glass!"

"Why not, Mother?"

"Because it's got liquor in it!"

"Oh, no, Mother, it's just ice and sugar when Mr. Pollitt's through with it."

"Honey, there's always a little liquor left in it."

"Oh, no, not a drop's left when Mr. Pollitt's through with it!"

"But you say there's sugar left in it, and, honey, you know that sugar is very absorbent."

"It's what, Mummy?"

"It absorbs some liquor and that's a good way to cul-

38

tivate a taste for it, and, honey, you know what dreadful consequences a taste for liquor can have. It's bad enough for a man, but for a woman it's fatal. So when you want ice and sugar, let Mother know and she'll prepare some for you, but don't ever let me catch you eating what's left in Mr. Pollitt's glass!"

"Mama?"

"Yes, precious?"

"It's almost completely dark now. Everybody is turning on their lights or driving out on the river road to cool off. Can't we go out riding in the electric?"

"No, honey, we can't till we know Mr. Pollitt's not —"

"Do you still think he will come?"

"Precious, how can I say? Is Mother a fortune-teller?"

"*Oh, here comes the Pierce, Mummy, here comes the Pierce!*"

"*Is it? Is it the Pierce?*"

"Oh, no. No, it isn't. It's a Hudson Super Six. Mummy, I'm going to pull up the wickets, now, and water the lawn, because if Mr. Pollitt does come, he'll have people with him or won't be in a condition to play croquet. And when I've finished, I want to drive the electric around the block."

"Drive it around the block, honey, but don't go into the business district with it."

"Are you going with me, Mummy?"

"No, precious, I'm going to sit here."

"It's cooler in the electric."

"I don't think so. The electric goes too slowly to make much breeze."

39

If Mr. Pollitt did finally arrive those evenings, it was likely to be with a caravan of cars that came from Memphis, and then Mrs. Grey would have to receive a raffish assortment of strangers as if she herself had invited them to a party. The party would not confine itself to the downstairs rooms and galleries but would explode quickly and brilliantly as a rocket in all directions, overflowing both floors of the house, spilling out upon the lawn and sometimes even penetrating the little building that housed the electric automobile and the oblong box that held the packed-away croquet set. On those party nights, the fantastically balustraded and gabled and turreted white building would glitter all over, like one of those huge night-excursion boats that came downriver from Memphis, and it would be full of ragtime music and laughter. But at some point in the evening there would be, almost invariably, a startling disturbance. Some male guest would utter a savage roar, a woman would scream, you would hear a shattering of glass. Almost immediately afterward, the lights would go out in the house, as if it really were a boat that had collided fatally with a shoal underwater. From all the doors and galleries and stairs, people would come rushing forth, and the dispersion would be more rapid than the arrival had been. A little while later, the police car would pull up in front of the house. The thin, pretty widow would come out on the front gallery to receive the chief of police, and you could hear her light voice tinkling like glass chimes, "Why, it was nothing, it was nothing at all, just somebody who drank a little too much and lost his temper. You know how that Memphis crowd is, Mr. Duggan, there's always one gentleman in it who can't hold his liquor. I know it's late, but we have such a huge lawn — it occupies half the block — that I shouldn't think anybody who wasn't overcome with curiosity would have to know that a party had been going on!"

And then something must have happened that made no sound at all.

It wasn't an actual death, but it had nearly all the external evidence of one. When death occurs in a house, the house is unnaturally quiet for a day or two before the occurrence is finished. During that interval, the enormous, translucent glass bell that seems to enclose and separate one house from those that surround it does not transmit any noise to those who are watching but seems to have thickened invisibly so that very little can be heard through it. That was the way it had been five months ago, when the pleasant young doctor had died of that fierce flower grown in his skull. It had been unnaturally quiet for several days, and then a peculiar gray car with frosted windows had crashed through the bell of silence and the young doctor had emerged from the house in a very curious way, as if he were giving a public demonstration of how to go to sleep on a narrow bed in atmosphere blazing with light and while in motion.

That was five months ago, and it was now early October.

The summer had spelled out a word that had no meaning, and the word was now spelled out and, with or without any meaning, there it was, inscribed with as heavy a touch as the signature of a miser on a check or a boy with chalk on a fence.

One afternoon, a fat and pleasantly smiling man, whom I had seen times without number loitering around in front of the used-car lot which adjoined the Paramount movie, came up the front walk of the Greys' with the excessive nonchalance of a man who is about to commit a robbery. He pushed the bell, waited awhile, pushed it again for a longer moment, and then was admitted through an opening that seemed to be hardly wide enough for his fingers. He came back out almost immediately with something caught in his fist. It was the key to the little building that contained the croquet set and the electric automobile. He entered that building and drew its folding doors all the way open to disclose the ladylike electric sitting there with its usual manner of a lady putting on or taking off her gloves at the entrance to a reception. He stared at it a moment, as if its elegance were momentarily baffling. But then he got in it and he drove it out of the garage, holding the polished black pilot stick with a look on his round face that was like the look of an adult who is a little embarrassed to find himself being amused by a game that was meant for children. He drove it serenely out into the wide, shady street and at an upstairs window of the house there was some kind of quick movement, as if a figure looking out had been startled by something it watched and then had retreated in haste . . .

Later, after the Greys had left town, I saw the elegant square vehicle, which appeared to be made out of glass and patent leather, standing with an air of haughty self-consciousness among a dozen or so other cars for sale in a lot called "Hi-Class Values" next door to the town's best movie, and as far as I know, it may be still sitting there, but many degrees less glittering by now.

The Greys were gone from Meridian all in one quick season: the young doctor whom everyone had liked in a hesitant, early way and had said would do well in the town with his understanding eyes and quiet voice; the thin, pretty woman, whom no one had really known except Brick Pollitt; and the plump little girl, who might someday be as pretty and slender as her mother. They had come and gone in one season, yes, like one of those tent shows that suddenly appear in a vacant lot in a southern town and cross the sky at night with mysteriously wheeling lights and unearthly music, and then are gone, and the summer goes on without them, as if they had never come there.

As for Mr. Brick Pollitt, I can remember seeing him only once after the Greys left town, for my time there was also of brief duration. This last time that I saw him was a brilliant fall morning. It was a Saturday morning in October. Brick's driver's license had been revoked again for some misadventure on the highway due to insufficient control of the wheel, and it was his legal wife, Margaret, who sat in the driver's seat of the Pierce-Arrow touring car. Brick did not sit beside her. He was on the back seat of the car, pitching this way and that way with the car's jolting motion, like a loosely wrapped package being delivered somewhere. Margaret Pollitt handled the car with a wonderful male assurance, her bare arms brown and muscular as a Negro field hand's, and the car's canvas top had been lowered the better to expose on its back seat the sheepishly grinning and nod-

ding figure of Brick Pollitt. He was clothed and bar-
bered with his usual immaculacy, so that he looked from
some distance like the president of a good social frater-
nity in a gentleman's college of the South. The knot of
his polka-dot tie was drawn as tight as strong and eager
fingers could knot a tie for an important occasion. One
of his large red hands protruded, clasping over the outside of the door to steady his motion, and on it glittered
two bands of gold, a small one about a finger, a large
one about the wrist. His cream-colored coat was neatly
folded on the seat beside him and he wore a shirt of
thin white material that was tinted faintly pink by his
skin beneath it. He was a man who had been, and even
at that time still was, the handsomest you were likely to
remember, physical beauty being of all human attributes
the most incontinently used and wasted, as if whoever
made it despised it, since it is made so often only to be
disgraced by painful degrees and drawn through the
streets in chains.

Margaret blew the car's silver trumpet at every inter-
section. She leaned this way and that way, elevating or
thrusting out an arm as she shouted gay greetings to
people on porches, merchants beside store entrances,
people she barely knew along the walks, calling them all
by their familiar names, as if she were running for office
in the town, while Brick nodded and grinned with senseless amiability behind her. It was exactly the way that
some ancient conqueror, such as Caesar or Alexander the
Great or Hannibal, might have led in chains through a
capital city the prince of a state newly conquered.

TWO ON A PARTY

TWO ON
A PARTY

HE couldn't really guess the age of the woman, Cora, but she was certainly not any younger than he, and he was almost thirty-five. There were some mornings when he thought she looked, if he wasn't flattering himself, almost old enough to be his mother, but there were evenings when the liquor was hitting her right, when her eyes were lustrous and her face becomingly flushed, and then she looked younger than he. As you get to know people, if you grow to like them, they begin to seem younger to you. The cruelty or damaging candor of the first impression is washed away like the lines in a doctored photograph, and Billy no longer remembered that the first night he met her he had thought of her as "an old bag." Of course, that night when he first met her she was not looking her best. It was in a Broadway bar; she was occupying the stool next to Billy and she had lost a diamond ear-clip and was complaining excitedly about it to the barman. She kept ducking down like a diving seal to look for it among the disgusting refuse under the brass rail, bobbing up and down and grunting and complaining, her face inflamed and swollen by the exertion, her rather heavy figure doubled into ludicrous positions. Billy had the uncomfortable feeling that she suspected him of stealing the diamond ear-clip. Each time she glanced at him his face turned hot. He always had that guilty feeling when anything valuable was lost, and it made him angry; he thought of her as an irritating old bag. Actually she wasn't accusing anybody of stealing the diamond ear-clip; in fact she kept assuring the barman that the clasp on the ear-clip was loose and she was a goddam fool to put it on.

Then Billy found the thing for her, just as he was about to leave the bar, embarrassed and annoyed beyond endurance; he noticed the sparkle of it almost under his shoe, the one on the opposite side from the ducking and puffing "old bag." With the sort of schoolteacherish austerity that he assumed when annoyed, when righteously indignant over something, an air that he had picked up during his short, much earlier, career as an English instructor at a midwestern university, he picked up the clip and slammed it wordlessly down on the bar in front of her and started to walk away. Two things happened to detain him. Three sailors off a Norwegian vessel came one, two, three through the revolving door of the bar and headed straight for the vacant stools just beyond where he had been sitting, and at the same instant, the woman, Cora, grabbed hold of his arm, shouting, Oh, don't go, don't go, the least you can do is let me buy you a drink! And so he had turned right around, as quickly and precisely as the revolving door through which the glittering trio of Norsemen had entered. Okay, why not? He resumed his seat beside her, she bought him a drink, he bought her a drink, inside of five minutes they were buying beer for the sailors and it was just as if the place was suddenly lit up by a dozen big chandeliers.

Quickly she looked different to him, not an old bag at all but really sort of attractive and obviously more to the taste of the dazzling Norsemen than Billy could be. Observing the two of them in the long bar mirror, himself and Cora, he saw that they looked good together, they made a good pair, they were mutually advantageous as a team for cruising the Broadway bars. She was a good deal darker than he and more heavily built. Billy was slight and he had very blond skin that the sun turned pink. Unfortunately for Billy, the pink also showed through the silky, thin yellow hair on the crown of his head where the baldness, so fiercely but impotently resisted, was now becoming a fact that he couldn't disown. Of course, the crown of the head doesn't show in the mirror unless you bow to your image in the glass, but there is no denying that the top of a queen's head is a conspicuous area on certain occasions which are not unimportant. That was how he put it, laughing about it to Cora. She said, Honey, I swear to Jesus I think you're more self-conscious about your looks and your age than I am! She said it kindly, in fact, she said everything kindly. Cora was a kind person. She was the kindest person that Billy had ever met. She said and meant everything kindly, literally everything; she hadn't a single malicious bone in her body, not a particle of jealousy or suspicion or evil in her nature, and that was what made it so sad that Cora was a lush. Yes, after he stopped thinking of her as "an old bag," which was almost immediately after they got acquainted, he started thinking of Cora as a lush, kindly, yes, but not as kindly as Cora thought about him, for Billy was not, by nature, as kind as Cora. Nobody else could be. Her kindness was monumental, the sort that simply doesn't exist any more, at least not in the queen world.

Fortunately for Billy, Billy was fairly tall. He had formed the defensive habit of holding his head rather high so that the crown of it wouldn't be so noticeable in bars, but unfortunately for Billy, he had what doctors had told him was a calcium deposit in the ears which made him hard of hearing and which could only be corrected by a delicate and expensive operation — boring a hole in the bone. He didn't have much money; he had just saved enough to live, not frugally but carefully, for two or three more years before he would have to go back to work at something. If he had the ear operation, he would have to go back to work right away and so abandon his sybaritic existence which suited him better than the dubious glory of being a somewhat better than hack writer of Hollywood film scenarios and so forth. Yes, and so forth!

Being hard of hearing, in fact, progressively so, he would have to crouch over and bend sidewise a little to hold a conversation in a bar, that is, if he wanted to understand what the other party was saying. In a bar it's dangerous not to listen to the other party, because the way of speaking is just as important as the look of the face in distinguishing between good trade and dirt, and Billy did not at all enjoy being beaten as some queens do. So he would have to bend sidewise and expose the almost baldness on the crown of his blond head, and he would cringe and turn red instead of pink with embarrassment as he did so. He knew that it was ridiculous of him to be that sensitive about it. But as he said to Cora, age does worse things to a queen than it does to a woman.

She disagreed about that and they had great arguments about it. But it was a subject on which Billy could hold forth as eloquently as a southern Senator making a filibuster against the repeal of the poll tax, and Cora would lose the argument by default, simply not able to continue it any longer, for Cora did not like gloomy topics of conversation so much as Billy liked them.

About her own defects of appearance, however, Cora was equally distressed and humble.

You see, she would tell him, I'm really a queen myself. I mean it's the same difference, honey, I like and do the same things, sometimes I think in bed if they're drunk enough they don't even know I'm a woman, at least they don't act like they do, and I don't blame them. Look at me, I'm a mess. I'm getting so heavy in the hips and I've got these big udders on me!

Nonsense, Billy would protest, you have a healthy and beautiful female body, and you mustn't low-rate yourself all the time that way, I won't allow it!

And he would place his arm about her warm and
Florida-sun-browned shoulders, exposed by her back-
less white gown (the little woolly-looking canary yellow
jacket being deposited on a vacant bar stool beside her),
for it was usually quite late, almost time for the bars to
close, when they began to discuss what the years had
done to them, the attritions of time. Beside Billy, too,
there would be a vacant bar stool on which he had
placed the hat that concealed his thinning hair from the
streets. It would be one of those evenings that gradually
wear out the exhilaration you start with. It would be
one of those evenings when lady luck showed the bitchy
streak in her nature. They would have had one or two
promising encounters which had fizzled out, coming
to a big fat zero at three A.M. In the game they played,
the true refinement of torture is to almost pull in a catch
and then the line breaks, and when that happens, each
not pitying himself as much as he did the other, they
would sit out the final hour before closing, talking about
the wicked things time had done to them, the gradual
loss of his hearing and his hair, the fatty expansion of
her breasts and buttocks, forgetting that they were still
fairly attractive people and still not old.

Actually, in the long run their luck broke about fifty-
fifty. Just about every other night one or the other of
them would be successful in the pursuit of what Billy
called "the lyric quarry." One or the other or both might
be successful on the good nights, and if it was a really
good night, then both would be. Good nights, that is,
really good nights, were by no means as rare as hen's
teeth nor were they as frequent as streetcars, but they

knew very well, both of them, that they did better together than they had done separately in the past. They
set off something warm and good in each other that
strangers responded to with something warm and good
in themselves. Loneliness dissolved any reserve and suspicion, the night was a great warm comfortable meeting
of people, it shone, it radiated, it had the effect of a dozen
big chandeliers, oh, it was great, it was grand, you simply couldn't describe it, you got the colored lights going,
and there it all was, the final pattern of it and the original pattern, all put together, made to fit exactly, no,
there were simply no words good enough to describe it.
And if the worst happened, if someone who looked like
a Botticelli angel drew a knife, or if the law descended
suddenly on you, and those were eventualities the possibility of which a queen must always consider, you still
could say you'd had a good run for your money.

Like everyone whose life is conditioned by luck, they
had some brilliant streaks of it and some that were dis-
mal. For instance, that first week they operated together
in Manhattan. That was really a freak; you couldn't
expect a thing like that to happen twice in a lifetime.
The trade was running as thick as spawning salmon up
those narrow cataracts in the Rockies. Head to tail, tail to
head, crowding, swarming together, seemingly driven
along by some immoderate instinct. It was not a question of catching; it was simply a question of deciding
which ones to keep and which to throw back in the
stream, all glittering, all swift, all flowing one way
which was toward you!

That week was in Manhattan, where they teamed up.

It was, to be exact, in Emerald Joe's at the corner of Forty-second and Broadway that they had met each other the night of the lost diamond clip that Billy had found. It was the week of the big blizzard and the big Chinese Red offensive in North Korea. The combination seemed to make for a wildness in the air, and trade is always best when the atmosphere of a city is excited whether it be over a national election or New Year's or a championship prizefight or the World Series baseball games; anything that stirs up the whole population makes it better for cruising.

Yes, it was a lucky combination of circumstances, and that first week together had been brilliant. It was before they started actually living together. At that time, she had a room at the Hotel Pennsylvania and he had one at the Astor. But at the end of that week, the one of their first acquaintance, they gave up separate establishments and took a place together at a small East Side hotel in the Fifties, because of the fact that Cora had an old friend from her hometown in Louisiana employed there as the night clerk. This one was a gay one that she had known long ago and innocently expected to be still the same. Cora did not understand how some people turn bitter. She had never turned bitchy and it was not understandable to her that others might. She said this friend on the desk was a perfect setup; he'd be delighted to see them bringing in trade. But that was the way in which it failed to work out . . .

That second week in New York was not a good one. Cora had been exceeding her usual quota of double ryes on the rocks and it began all at once to tell on her appearance. Her system couldn't absorb any more; she had reached the saturation point, and it was no longer possible for her to pick herself up in the evenings. Her face had a bloated look and her eyes remained bloodshot all the time. They looked, as she said, like a couple of poached eggs in a sea of blood, and Billy had to agree with her that they did. She started looking her oldest and she had the shakes.

Then about Friday of that week the gay one at the desk turned bitchy on them. Billy had expected him to turn, but Cora hadn't. Sooner or later, Billy knew, that frustrated queen was bound to get a severe attack of jaundice over the fairly continual coming and going of so much close-fitting blue wool, and Billy was not mistaken. When they brought their trade in, he would slam down the key without looking at them or speaking a word of greeting. Then one night they brought in a perfectly divine-looking pharmacist's mate of Italian extraction and his almost equally attractive buddy. The old friend of Cora's exploded, went off like a spit-devil.

I'm sorry, he hissed, but this is *not* a flea-bag! You should have stayed on Times Square where you started.

There was a scene. He refused to give them their room-key unless the two sailors withdrew from the lobby. Cora said, Fuck you, Mary, and reached across the desk and grabbed the key from the hook. The old friend seized her wrist and tried to make her let go.

Put that key down, he shrieked, or you'll be sorry!

He started twisting her wrist; then Billy hit him; he vaulted right over the desk and knocked the son-of-a-bitch into the switchboard.

Call the police, call the police, the clerk screamed to the porter.

Drunk as she was, Cora suddenly pulled herself together. She took as much command of the situation as could be taken.

You boys wait outside, she said to the sailors, there's no use in you all getting into S.P. trouble.

One of them, the Italian, wanted to stay and join in the roughhouse, but his buddy, who was the bigger one, forcibly removed him to the sidewalk. (Cora and Billy never saw them again.) By that time, Billy had the night clerk by the collar and was giving him slaps that bobbed his head right and left like something rubber, as if that night clerk was everything that he loathed in a hostile world. Cora stopped him. She had that wonderful, that really invaluable faculty of sobering up in a crisis. She pulled Billy off her old friend and tipped the colored porter ten dollars not to call in the law. She turned on all her southern charm and sweetness, trying to straighten things out. You darling, she said, you poor darling, to the bruised night clerk. The law was not called, but the outcome of the situation was far from pleasant. They had to check out, of course, and the hysterical old friend said he was going to write Cora's family in Alexandria, Louisiana, and give them a factual report on how she was living here in New York and how he supposed she was living anywhere else since she'd left home and he knew her.

At that time Billy knew almost nothing about Cora's background and former life, and he was surprised at her being so upset over this hysterical threat, which seemed unimportant to him. But all the next day Cora kept alluding to it, speculating whether or not the bitch would really do it, and it was probably on account of this threat that Cora made up her mind to leave New York. It was the only time, while they were living together, that Cora ever made a decision, at least about places to go and when to go to them. She had none of that desire to manage and dominate which is a typically American perversion of the female nature. As Billy said to himself, with that curious harshness of his toward things he loved, she was like a big piece of seaweed. Sometimes he said it irritably to himself, just like a big piece of seaweed washing this way and that way. It isn't healthy or normal to be so passive, Billy thought.

Where do you want to eat?

I don't care.

No, tell me, Cora, what place would you prefer?

I really don't care, she'd insist, it makes no difference to me.

Sometimes out of exasperation he would say, All right, let's eat at the Automat.

Only then would Cora demur.

Of course, if you want to, honey, but couldn't we eat some place with a liquor license?

She was agreeable to anything and everything; she seemed to be grateful for any decision made for her, but this one time, when they left New York, when they made their first trip together, it was Cora's decision to go. This was before Billy began to be terribly fond of Cora, and at first, when Cora said, Honey, I've got to leave this town or Hugo (the hotel queen) will bring up

Bobo (her brother who was a lawyer in Alexandria and who had played some very unbrotherly legal trick on her when a certain inheritance was settled) and there will be hell to pay, he will freeze up my income — then, at this point, Billy assumed that they would go separate ways. But at the last moment Billy discovered that he didn't want to go back to a stag existence. He discovered that solitary cruising had been lonely, that there were spiritual comforts as well as material advantages in their double arrangement. No matter how bad luck was, there was no longer such a thing as going home by himself to the horrors of a second- or third-class hotel bedroom. Then there *were* the material advantages, the fact they actually did better operating together, and the fact that it was more economical. Billy had to be somewhat mean about money since he was living on savings that he wanted to stretch as far as he could, and Cora more than carried her own weight in the expense department. She was only too eager to pick up a check and Billy was all too willing to let her do it. She spoke of her income but she was vague about what it was or came from. Sometimes looking into her handbag she had a fleeting expression of worry that made Billy wonder uncomfortably if her finances, like his, might not be continually dwindling toward an eventual point of eclipse. But neither of them had a provident nature or dared to stop and consider much of the future.

Billy was a light traveler, all he carried with him was a three-suiter, a single piece of hand luggage and his portable typewriter. When difficulties developed at a hotel, he could clear out in five minutes or less. He rubbed his chin for a minute, then he said, Cora, how about me going with you?

They shared a compartment in the Sunshine Special to Florida. Why to Florida? One of Cora's very few pretensions was a little command of French; she was fond of using little French phrases which she pronounced badly. Honey, she said, I have a little *pied-à-terre* in Florida.

Pied-à-terre was one of those little French phrases that she was proud of using, and she kept talking about it, her little *pied-à-terre* in the Sunshine State.

Whereabouts is it, Billy asked her.

No place fashionable, she told him, but just you wait and see and you might be surprised and like it.

That night in the shared compartment of the Pullman was the first time they had sex together. It happened casually, it was not important and it was not very satisfactory, perhaps because they were each too anxious to please the other, each too afraid the other would be disappointed. Sex has to be slightly selfish to have real excitement. Start worrying about the other party's reactions and the big charge just isn't there, and you've got to do it a number of times together before it becomes natural enough to be a completely satisfactory thing. The first time between strangers can be like a blaze of light, but when it happens between people who know each other well and have an established affection, it's likely to be self-conscious and even a little embarrassing, most of all afterwards.

Afterwards they talked about it with a slight sense of strain. They felt they had gotten that sort of thing squared away and would not have to think about it between them again. But perhaps, in a way, it did add a little something to the intimacy of their living together; at least it had, as they put it, squared things away a bit. And they talked about it shyly, each one trying too hard to flatter the other.

Gee, honey, said Cora, you're a wonderful lay, you've got wonderful skin, smooth as a baby's, gee, it sure was wonderful, honey, I enjoyed it so much, I wish you had. But I know you didn't like it and it was selfish of me to start it with you.

You didn't like it, he said.

I swear I *loved* it, she said, but I knew that *you* didn't like it, so we won't do it again.

He told Cora that she was a wonderful lay and that he had loved it every bit as much as she did and maybe more, but he agreed they'd better not do it again.

Friends can't be lovers, he said.

No, they can't, she agreed with a note of sadness.

Then jealousy enters in.

Yes, they get jealous and bitchy . . .

They never did it again, at least not that completely, not any time during the year and two months since they started living together. Of course, there were some very drunk, *blind* drunk nights when they weren't quite sure what happened between them after they fell into bed, but you could be pretty certain it wasn't a sixty-six in that condition. Sixty-six was Cora's own slightly inexact term for a normal lay, that is, a lay that occurred in the ordinary position.

What happened? Billy would ask when she'd had a party.

Oh, it was wonderful, she would exclaim, a sixty-six!

Good Jesus, drunk as he was?

Oh, I sobered him up, she'd laugh.

And what did you do, Billy? Take the sheets? Ha ha, you'll have to leave this town with a board nailed over your ass!

Sometimes they had a serious conversation, though most of the time they tried to keep the talk on a frivolous plane. It troubled Cora to talk about serious matters, probably because matters were too serious to be talked about with comfort. And for the first month or so neither of them knew that the other one actually had a mind that you could talk to. Gradually they discovered about each other the other things, and although it was always their mutual pursuit, endless and indefatigable, of "the lyric quarry" that was the mainstay of their relationship, at least upon its surface, the other things, the timid and tender values that can exist between people, began to come shyly out and they had a respect for each other, not merely to like and enjoy, as neither had ever respected another person.

It was a rare sort of moral anarchy, doubtless, that held them together, a really fearful shared hatred of everything that was restrictive and which they felt to be false in the society they lived in and against the grain of which they continually operated. They did not dislike what they called "squares." They loathed and despised them, and for the best of reasons. Their existence was a never-ending contest with the squares of the world, the squares who have such a virulent rage at everything not in their book. Getting around the squares, evading, defying the phony rules of convention, that was maybe responsible for half their pleasure in their outlaw existence. They were a pair of kids playing cops and robbers; except for that element, the thrill of something lawless, they probably would have gotten bored with cruising. Maybe not, maybe so. Who can tell? But hotel clerks and house dicks and people in adjoining hotel bedrooms, the specter of Cora's family in Alexandria, Louisiana, the specter of Billy's family in Montgomery, Alabama, the various people involved in the niggardly control of funds, almost everybody that you passed when you were drunk and hilariously gay on the street, especially all those bull-like middle-aged couples that stood off sharply and glared at you as you swept through a hotel lobby with your blushing trade — all, all, all of those were natural enemies to them, as well as the one great terrible, worst of all enemies, which is the fork-tailed, cloven-hoofed, pitchfork-bearing devil of Time!

Time, of course, was the greatest enemy of all, and they knew that each day and each night was cutting down a little on the distance between the two of them running together and that demon pursuer. And knowing it, knowing that nightmarish fact, gave a wild sort of sweetness of despair to their two-ring circus.

And then, of course, there was also the fact that Billy was, or had been at one time, a sort of artist *manqué* and still had a touch of homesickness for what that was.

Sometime, said Cora, you're going to get off the party.

Why should I get off the party?

Because you're a serious person. You are fundamentally a serious sort of a person.

I'm not a serious person any more than you are. I'm a goddam remittance man and you know it.

No, I don't know it, said Cora. Remittance men get letters enclosing checks, but you don't even get letters.

Billy rubbed his chin.

Then how do you think I live?

Ha ha, she said.

What does 'Ha Ha' mean?

It means I know what I know!

Balls, said Billy, you know no more about me than I do about you.

I know, said Cora, that you used to write for a living, and that for two years you haven't been writing but you're still living on the money you made as a writer, and sooner or later, you're going to get off the party and go back to working again and being a serious person. What do you imagine I think of that portable typewriter you drag around with you everywhere we go, and that big fat portfolio full of papers you tote underneath your shirts in your three-suiter? I wasn't born yesterday or the day before yesterday, baby, and I know that you're going to get off the party some day and leave me on it.

If I get off the party, we'll get off it together, said Billy.

And me do *what?* she'd ask him, realistically.

And he would not be able to answer that question. For she knew and he knew, both of them knew it together, that they would remain together only so long as they stayed on the party, and not any longer than that. And in his heart he knew, much as he might deny it, that it would be pretty much as Cora predicted in her Cassandra moods. One of those days or nights it was bound to happen. He would get off the party, yes, he would certainly be the one of them to get off it, because there was really nothing for Cora to do but stay on it. Of course, if she broke down, that would take her off it. Usually or almost always it's only a breakdown that takes you off a party. A party is like a fast-moving train — you can't jump off it, it thunders past the stations you might get off at, very few people have the courage to leap from a thing that is moving that fast, they have to stay with it no matter where it takes them. It only stops when it crashes, the ticker wears out, a blood vessel bursts, the liver or kidneys quit working. But Cora was tough. Her system had absorbed a lot of punishment, but from present appearances it was going to absorb a lot more. She was too tough to crack up any time soon, but she was not tough enough to make the clean break, the daring jump off, that Billy knew, or felt that he knew, that he was still able to make when he was ready to make it. Cora was five or maybe even ten years older than Billy. She rarely looked it, but she was that much older and time is one of the biggest differences between two people.

I've got news for you, baby, and you had better believe it.

What news?

This news, Cora would say. You're going to get off the party and leave me on it!

Well, it was probably true, as true as anything is, and what a pity it was that Cora was such a grand person.

If she had not been such a nice person, so nice that at first you thought it must be phony and only gradually came to see it was real, it wouldn't matter so much. For usually queens fall out like a couple of thieves quarreling over the split of the loot. Billy remembered the one in Baton Rouge who was so annoyed when he confiscated a piece she had a lech for that she made of Billy an effigy of candle wax and stuck pins in it with dreadful imprecations, kept the candle-wax effigy on her mantel and performed black rites before it. But Cora was not like that. She didn't have a jealous bone in her body. She took as much pleasure in Billy's luck as her own. Sometimes he suspected she was more interested in Billy having good luck than having it herself.

Sometimes Billy would wonder. Why do we do it?

We're lonely people, she said, I guess it's as simple as that . . .

But nothing is ever quite so simple as it appears when you are comfortably loaded.

Take this occasion, for instance.

Billy and Cora are traveling by motor. The automobile is a joint possession which they acquired from a used-car dealer in Galveston. It is a '47 Buick convertible with a brilliant new scarlet paint-job. Cora and Billy are outfitted with corresponding brilliance; she has on a pair of black and white checked slacks, a cowboy shirt with a bucking broncho over one large breast and a roped steer over the other, and she has on harlequin sun-glasses with false diamonds encrusting the rims. Her freshly peroxided hair is bound girlishly on top of her head with a diaphanous scarf of magenta chiffon;

she has on her diamond ear-clips and her multiple slave-bracelets, three of them real gold and two of them only gold-plated, and hundreds of little tinkling gold attachments, such as tiny footballs, liberty bells, hearts, mandolins, choo-choos, sleds, tennis rackets, and so forth. Billy thinks she has overdone it a little. It must be admitted, however, that she is a noticeable person, especially at the wheel of this glittering scarlet Roadmaster. They have swept down the Camino Real, the Old Spanish Trail, from El Paso eastward instead of westward, having decided at the last moment to resist the allure of Southern California on the other side of the Rockies and the desert, since it appears that the Buick has a little tendency to overheat and Cora notices that the oil pressure is not what it should be. So they have turned eastward instead of westward, with a little side trip to Corpus Christi to investigate the fact or fancy of those legendary seven connecting glory-holes in a certain tearoom there. It turned out to be fancy or could not be located. Says Cora: You queens know places but never know where places are!

A blowout going into New Orleans. That's to be expected, said Cora, they never give you good rubber. The spare is no good either. Two new tires had to be bought in New Orleans and Cora paid for them by hocking some of her baubles. There was some money left over and she buys Billy a pair of cowboy boots. They are still on the Wild West kick. Billy also presents a colorful appearance in a pair of blue jeans that fit as if they had been painted on him, the fancily embossed cowboy boots and a sport shirt that is covered with leaping dolphins,

66

Ha ha! They have never had so much fun in their life together, the colored lights are going like pinwheels on the Fourth of July, everything is big and very bright celebration. The Buick appears to be a fairly solid investment, once it has good rubber on it and they get those automatic devices to working again . . .

It is a mechanical age that we live in, they keep saying.

They did Mobile, Pensacola, West Palm Beach and Miami in one continual happy breeze! The scoreboard is brilliant! Fifteen lays, all hitching rides on the highway, since they got the convertible. It's all we ever needed to hit the jackpot, Billy exults . . .

Then comes the badman into the picture!

They are on the Florida keys, just about midway between the objective, Key West, and the tip of the peninsula. Nothing is visible about them but sky and mangrove swamp. Then all of a sudden that used-car dealer in Galveston pulls the grinning joker out of his sleeve. Under the hood of the car comes a loud metallic noise as if steel blades are scraping. The fancy heap will not take the gas. It staggers gradually to a stop, and trying to start it again succeeds only in running the battery down. Moreover, the automatic top has ceased to function; it is the meridian of a day in early spring which is as hot as midsummer on the Florida keys . . .

Cora would prefer to make light of the situation, if Billy would let her do so. The compartment of the dashboard is filled with roadmaps, a flashlight and a thermos of dry martinis. The car has barely uttered its expiring rattle and gasp when Cora's intensely ornamented arm reaches out for this unfailing simplification of the human dilemma. For the first time in their life together, Billy interferes with her drinking, and out of pure meanness. He grabs her wrist and restrains her. He is suddenly conscious of how disgusted he is with what he calls her Oriental attitude toward life. The purchase of this hoax was her idea. Two thirds of the investment was also her money. Moreover she had professed to be a pretty good judge of motors. Billy himself had frankly confessed that he couldn't tell a spark plug from a carburetor. So it was Cora who had examined and appraised the possible buys on the used-car lots of Galveston and come upon this 'bargain'! She had looked under the hoods and shimmied fatly under the chassis of dozens of cars before she arrived at this remarkably misguided choice. The car had been suspiciously cheap for a '47 Roadmaster with such a brilliantly smart appearance, but Cora said it was just as sound as the American dollar! She put a thousand dollars into the deal and Billy put in five hundred which had come in from the resale to pocket editions of a lurid potboiler he had written under a pseudonym a number of years ago when he was still an active member of the literary profession.

Now Cora was reaching into the dashboard compartment for a thermos of martinis because the car whose purchase was her responsibility had collapsed in the middle of nowhere . . .

Billy seizes her wrist and twists it.

Let go of that goddam thermos, you're not gonna get drunk!

She struggles with him a little, but soon she gives up and suddenly goes feminine and starts to cry.

68

After that a good while passes in which they sit side by side in silence in the leather-lined crematorium of the convertible.

A humming sound begins to be heard in the distance. Perhaps it's a motorboat on the other side of the mangroves, perhaps something on the highway . . .

Cora begins to jingle and jangle as she twists her ornamented person this way and that way with nervous henlike motions of the head and shoulder and torso, peering about on both sides and half rising and flopping awkwardly back down again, and finally grunting eagerly and piling out of the car, losing her balance, sprawling into a ditch, ha ha, scrambling up again, taking the middle of the road and making great frantic circles with her arms as a motorcycle approaches. If the cyclist had desired to pass them it would have been hardly possible. Later Billy will remind her that it was *she* who stopped it. But right now Billy is enchanted, not merely at the prospect of a rescue but much more by the looks of the potential instrument of rescue. The motorcyclist is surely something dispatched from a sympathetic region back of the sun. He has one of those blond and block-shaped heads set upon a throat which is as broad as the head itself and has the smooth and supple muscularity of the male organ in its early stage of tumescence. This bare throat and the blond head above it have never been in a country where the sun is distant. The hands are enormous square knobs to the golden doors of Paradise. And the legs that straddle the quiescent fury of the cycle (called Indian) could not have been better designed by the appreciative eyes and fingers of Michelangelo or Phidias or Rodin. It is in the direct and pure line of those who have witnessed and testified in stone what they have seen of a simple physical glory in mankind! The eyes are behind sun-glasses. Cora is a good judge of eyes but she has to see them to judge them. Sometimes she will say to a young man wearing sun-glasses, Will you kindly uncover the windows of your soul? She considers herself to be a better judge of good and bad trade than is Billy whose record contains a number of memorable errors. Later Cora will remember that from the moment she saw this youth on the motorcycle something whispered *Watch Out* in her ear. Honey, she will say, later, he had more Stop signs on him than you meet when you've got five minutes to get to the station! Perhaps this will be an exaggerated statement, but it is true that Cora had misgivings in exact proportion to Billy's undisguised enchantment.

As for right now, the kid seems fairly obliging. He swings his great legs off the cycle which he rests upon a metal support. He hardly says anything. He throws back the hood of the car and crouches into it for a couple of minutes, hardly more than that, then the expressionless blond cube comes back into view and announces without inflection, Bearings gone out.

What does that mean, asks Cora.

That means you been screwed, he says.

What can we do about it?

Not a goddam thing. You better junk it.

What did he say, inquires Billy.

He said, Cora tells him, that the bearings have gone out.

What are bearings?

The cyclist utters a short barking laugh. He is back astraddle the frankly shaped leather seat of his Indian, but Cora has once more descended from the Buick and she has resorted to the type of flirtation that even most queens would think common. She has fastened her bejeweled right hand over the elevated and narrow front section of the saddle which the boy sits astride. There is not only proximity but contact between their two parties, and all at once the boy's blond look is both contemptuous and attentive, and his attitude toward their situation has undergone a drastic alteration. He is now engaged in it again.

There's a garage on Boca Raton, he tells them. I'll see if they got a tow truck. I think they got one.

Off he roars down the Keys!

One hour and forty-five minutes later the abdicated Roadmaster is towed into a garage on Boca Raton, and Cora and Billy plus their new-found acquaintance are checking, all three, into a tourist cabin at a camp called The Idle-wild, which is across the highway from the garage.

Cora has thought to remove her thermos of martinis from the dashboard compartment, and this time Billy has not offered any objection. Billy is restored to good spirits. Cora still feels guilty, profoundly and abjectly guilty, about the purchase of the glittering fraud, but she is putting up a good front. She knows, however, that Billy will never quite forgive and forget and she does not understand why she made that silly profession of knowing so much about motors. It was, of course, to impress her beloved companion. He knows so much more than she about so many things, she has to pretend, now and then, to know *something* about *something*, even when she knows in her heart that she is a comprehensive and unabridged dictionary of human ignorance on nearly all things of importance. She sighs in her heart because she's become a pretender, and once you have pretended, is it ever possible to stop pretending?

Pretending to be a competent judge of a motor has placed her in the sad and embarrassing position of having cheated Billy out of five hundred dollars. How can she make it up to him?

A whisper in the heart of Cora: *I love him!*

Whom does she love?

There are three persons in the cabin, herself, and Billy and the young man from the highway.

Cora despises herself and she has never been much attracted to men of an altogether physical type.

So there is the dreadful answer! She is in love with Billy!

I am in love with Billy, she whispers to herself.

That acknowledgment seems to call for a drink.

She gets up and pours herself another martini. Unfortunately someone, probably Cora herself, has forgotten to screw the cap back on the thermos bottle and the drinks are now tepid. No drink is better than an ice-cold martini, but no drink is worse than a martini getting warm. However, be that as it may, the discovery just made, the one about loving Billy, well, after *that* one the temperature of a drink is not so important so long as the stuff is still liquor!

She says to herself: I have admitted a fact! Well, the only thing to do with a fact is admit it, but once admitted, you don't have to keep harping on it.

Never again, so long as she stays on the party with her companion, will she put into words her feelings for him, not even in the privacy of her heart . . .

Le coeur a ses raisons que la raison ne connaît pas!

That is one of those little French sayings that Cora is proud of knowing and often repeats to herself as well as to others.

Sometimes she will translate it, to those who don't know the French language, as follows:

The heart knows the scoop when the brain is ignorant of it!

Ha ha!

Well, now she is back in the cabin after a mental excursion that must have lasted at least a half an hour.

Things have progressed thus far.

Billy has stripped down to his shorts and he has persuaded the square-headed blond to do likewise.

Cora herself discovers that she has made concessions to the unseasonable warmth of the little frame building.

All she is wearing is her panties and bra.

She looks across without real interest at the square-headed stranger. Yes. A magnificent torso, as meaningless, now, to Cora as a jigsaw puzzle which put together exhibits a cow munching grass in a typical one-tree pasture . . .

Excuse me, people, she remarks to Billy. I just remembered I promised to make a long-distance call to Atlanta.

A long-distance call to Atlanta is a code message between herself and Billy.

What it means is this: The field is yours to conquer!

Cora goes out, having thrown on a jacket and pulled on her checkerboard slacks.

Where does Cora go? Not far, not far at all.

She is leaning against a palm tree not more than five yards distant from the cabin. She is smoking a cigarette in a shadow.

Inside the cabin the field is Billy's to conquer.

Billy says to the cyclist: How do you like me?

Huh . . .

(That is the dubious answer to his question!)

Billy gives him a drink, another one, thinking that this may evoke a less equivocal type of response.

How do you like me, now?

You want to know how I like you?

Yes!

I like you the way that a cattleman loves a sheep-herder!

I am not acquainted, says Billy, with the likes and dislikes of men who deal in cattle.

Well, says the square-headed blond, if you keep messing around I'm going to give you a demonstration of it!

A minute is a microscope view of eternity.

It is less than a minute before Cora hears a loud sound.

She knew what it was before she even heard it, and almost before she heard it, that thud of a body not falling but thrown to a floor, she is back at the door of the cabin and pushing it open and returning inside.

Hello! is what she says with apparent good humor.

She does not seem to notice Billy's position and bloody mouth on the floor . . .

Well, she says, I got my call through to Atlanta!

While she is saying this, she is getting out of her jacket and checkerboard slacks, and she is not stopping there.

Instant diversion is the doctor's order.

She is stripped bare in ten seconds, and on the bed.

Billy has gotten outside and she is enduring the most undesired embrace that she can remember in all her long history of desired and undesired and sometimes only patiently borne embraces . . .

Why do we do it?

We're lonely people. I guess it's simple as that . . .

But nothing is ever that simple! Don't you know it?

AND so the story continues where it didn't leave off . . .

Trade ceased to have much distinction. One piece was fundamentally the same as another, and the nights were like waves rolling in and breaking and retreating again and leaving you washed up on the wet sands of morning.

Something continual and something changeless.

The sweetness of their living together persisted.

We're friends! said Cora.

She meant a lot more than that, but Billy is satisfied with this spoken definition, and there's no other that can safely be framed in language.

Sometimes they look about them, privately and together, and what they see is something like what you see through a powerful telescope trained upon the moon, flatly illuminated craters and treeless plains and a vacancy of light — much light, but an emptiness in it.

Calcium is the element of this world.

Each has held some private notion of death. Billy thinks his death is going to be violent. Cora thinks hers will be ungraciously slow. Something will surrender by painful inches . . .

Meanwhile they are together.

To Cora that's the one important thing left.

Cities!

You queens know places, but never know where places are!

No Mayor has ever handed them a gold key, nor have they entered under a silken banner of welcome, but they have gone to them all in the northern half of the western hemisphere, this side of the Arctic Circle! Ha ha, just about all . . .

Many cities!

Sometimes they wake up early to hear the awakening tumult of a city and to reflect upon it.

They're two on a party which has made a departure and a rather wide one.

Into brutality? No. It's not that simple.

Into vice? No. It isn't nearly that simple.

Into what, then?

Into something unlawful? Yes, of course!

But in the night, hands clasping and no questions asked.

In the morning, a sense of being together no matter what comes, and the knowledge of not having struck nor lied nor stolen.

A female lush and a fairy who travel together, who are two on a party, and the rush continues.

They wake up early, sometimes, and hear the city coming awake, the increase of traffic, the murmurous shuffle of crowds on their way to their work, the ordinary resumption of daytime life in a city, and they reflect upon it a little from their, shall we say, bird's-eye situation.

There's the radio and the newspaper and there is TV, which Billy says means 'Tired Vaudeville,' and everything that is known is known very fully and very fully stated.

But after all, when you reflect upon it at the only time that is suitable for reflection, what can you do but turn your other cheek to the pillow?

Two queens sleeping together with sometimes a stranger between them . . .

One morning a phone will ring.

Cora will answer, being the lighter sleeper and the quicker to rise.

Bad news!

Clapping a hand over the shrill mouthpiece, instinctive gesture of secrecy, she will cry to Billy.

Billy, Billy, wake up! They've raided the Flamingo! The heat is on! Get packed!

Almost gaily this message is delivered and the packing performed, for it's fun to fly away from a threat of danger.

(Most dreams are about it, one form of it or another, in which man remembers the distant mother with wings . . .)

Off they go, from Miami to Jacksonville, from Jacksonville to Savannah or Norfolk, all winter shuttling about the Dixie circuit, in spring going back to Manhattan, two birds flying together against the wind, nothing real but the party, and even that sort of dreamy.

In the morning, always Cora's voice addressing room service, huskily, softly, not to disturb his sleep before the coffee arrives, and then saying gently, Billy, Billy, your coffee . . .

Cup and teaspoon rattling like castanets as she hands it to him, often spilling a little on the bedclothes and saying, Oh, honey, excuse me, ha ha!

THE RESEMBLANCE BETWEEN A
VIOLIN CASE AND A COFFIN

*Inscribed to the memory of
Isabel Sevier Williams*

The Resemblance
BETWEEN A
VIOLIN CASE
AND A COFFIN

With her advantage of more than two years and
the earlier maturity of girls, my sister moved before me
into that country of mysterious differences where children grow up. And although we naturally continued
to live in the same house, she seemed to have gone on a
journey while she remained in sight. The difference
came about more abruptly than you would think possible, and it was vast, it was like the two sides of the
Sunflower River that ran through the town where we
lived. On one side was a wilderness where giant cypresses
seemed to engage in mute rites of reverence at the edge
of the river, and the blurred pallor of the Dobyne place
that used to be a plantation, now vacant and seemingly
ravaged by some impalpable violence fiercer than flames,

and back of this dusky curtain, the immense cotton-fields that absorbed the whole visible distance in one sweeping gesture. But on the other side, avenues, commerce, pavements and homes of people: those two, separated by only a yellowish, languorous stream that you could throw a rock over. The rumbling wooden bridge that divided, or joined, those banks was hardly shorter than the interval in which my sister moved away from me. Her look was startled, mine was bewildered and hurt. Either there was no explanation or none was permitted between the one departing and the one left behind. The earliest beginning of it that I can remember was one day when my sister got up later than usual with an odd look, not as if she had been crying, although perhaps she had, but as though she had received some painful or frightening surprise, and I observed an equally odd difference in the manner toward her of my mother and grandmother. She was escorted to the kitchen table for breakfast as though she were in danger of toppling over on either side, and everything was handed to her as though she could not reach for it. She was addressed in hushed and solicitous voices, almost the way that docile servants speak to an employer. I was baffled and a little disgusted. I received no attention at all, and the one or two glances given me by my sister had a peculiar look of resentment in them. It was as if I had struck her the night before and given her a bloody nose or a black eye, except that she wore no bruise, no visible injury, and there had been no altercation between us in recent days. I spoke to her several times, but for some reason she ignored my remarks, and when I became irritated and

82

yelled at her, my grandmother suddenly reached over and twisted my ear, which was one of the few times that I can remember when she ever offered me more than the gentlest reproach. It was a Saturday morning, I remember, of a hot yellow day and it was the hour when my sister and I would ordinarily take to the streets on our wheels. But the custom was now disregarded. After breakfast my sister appeared somewhat strengthened but still alarmingly pale and as silent as ever. She was then escorted to the parlor and encouraged to sit down at the piano. She spoke in a low whimpering tone to my grandmother who adjusted the piano stool very carefully and placed a cushion on it and even turned the pages of sheet music for her as if she were incapable of finding the place for herself. She was working on a simple piece called *The Aeolian Harp*, and my grandmother sat beside her while she played, counting out the tempo in a barely audible voice, now and then reaching out to touch the wrists of my sister in order to remind her to keep them arched. Upstairs my mother began to sing to herself which was something she only did when my father had just left on a long trip with his samples and would not be likely to return for quite a while, and my grandfather, up since daybreak, was mumbling a sermon to himself in the study. All was peaceful except my sister's face. I did not know whether to go outside or stay in. I hung around the parlor a little while, and finally I said to Grand, Why can't she practice later? As if I had made some really brutal remark, my sister jumped up in tears and fled to her upstairs bedroom. What was the matter with her? My grandmother said,

Your sister is not well today. She said it gently and gravely, and then she started to follow my sister upstairs, and I was deserted. I was left alone in the very uninteresting parlor. The idea of riding alone on my wheel did not please me for often when I did that, I was set upon by the rougher boys of the town who called me Preacher and took a peculiar delight in asking me obscene questions that would embarrass me to the point of nausea . . .

In this way was instituted the time of estrangement that I could not understand. From that time on the division between us was ever more clearly established. It seemed that my mother and grandmother were approving and conspiring to increase it. They had never before bothered over the fact that I had depended so much on the companionship of my sister but now they were continually asking me why I did not make friends with other children. I was ashamed to tell them that other children frightened me nor was I willing to admit that my sister's wild imagination and inexhaustible spirits made all other substitute companions seem like the shadows of shades, for now that she had abandoned me, mysteriously and willfully withdrawn her enchanting intimacy, I felt too resentful even to acknowledge secretly, to myself, how much had been lost through what she had taken away . . .

Sometimes I think she might have fled back into the more familiar country of childhood if she had been allowed to, but the grown-up ladies of the house, and even the colored girl, Ozzie, were continually telling her that such and such a thing was not proper for her to

84

do. It was not proper for my sister not to wear stockings or to crouch in the yard at a place where the earth was worn bare to bounce a rubber ball and scoop up starry-pointed bits of black metal called jacks. It was not even proper for me to come into her room without knocking. All of these proprieties struck me as mean and silly and perverse, and the wound of them turned me inward.

My sister had been magically suited to the wild country of childhood but it remained to be seen how she would adapt herself to the uniform and yet more complex world that grown girls enter. I suspect that I have defined that world incorrectly with the word uniform; later, yes, it becomes uniform, it straightens out into an all too regular pattern. But between childhood and adulthood there is a broken terrain which is possibly even wilder than childhood was. The wilderness is interior. The vines and the brambles seem to have been left behind but actually they are thicker and more confusing, although they are not so noticeable from the outside. Those few years of dangerous passage are an ascent into unknown hills. They take the breath sometimes and bewilder the vision. My mother and maternal grandmother came of a calmer blood than my sister and I. They were unable to suspect the hazards that we were faced with, having in us the turbulent blood of our father. Irreconcilables fought for supremacy in us; peace could never be made: at best a smoldering sort of armistice might be reached after many battles. Childhood had held those clashes in abeyance. They were somehow timed to explode at adolescence, silently, shaking the earth where we were standing. My sister now felt those tremors under her feet. It seemed to me that a shadow had fallen on her. Or had it fallen on me, with her light at a distance? Yes, it was as if someone had carried a lamp into another room that I could not enter. I watched her from a distance and under a shadow. And looking back on it now, I see that those two or three years when the fatal dice were still in the tilted box, were the years of her beauty. The long copperish curls which had swung below her shoulders, bobbing almost constantly with excitement, were unexpectedly removed one day, an afternoon of a day soon after the one when she had fled from the piano in reasonless tears. Mother took her downtown. I was not allowed to go with them but was told once more to find someone else to play with. And my sister returned without her long copper curls. It was like a formal acknowledgment of the sorrowful differences and division which had haunted the house for some time. I noted as she came in the front door that she had now begun to imitate the walk of grown ladies, the graceful and quick and decorous steps of my mother, and that she kept her arms at her sides instead of flung out as if brushing curtains aside as she sprang forward in the abruptly lost days. But there was much more than that. When she entered the parlor, at the fading hour of the afternoon, it was as momentous as if brass horns had sounded, she wore such beauty. Mother came after her looking flushed with excitement and my grandmother descended the stairs with unusual lightness. They spoke in hushed voices. Astonishing, said my mother. She's like Isabel. This was the name of a sister of my father's who was a famed beauty in Knoxville. She was probably the one woman in the world of whom my mother was intimidated, and our occasional summer journeys to Knoxville from the Delta of Mississippi were like priestly tributes to a seat of holiness, for though my mother would certainly never make verbal acknowledgment of my aunt's superiority in matters of taste and definitions of quality, it was nevertheless apparent that she approached Knoxville and my father's younger sister in something very close to fear and trembling. Isabel had a flame, there was no doubt about it, a lambency which, once felt, would not fade from the eyes. It had an awful quality, as though it shone outward while it burned inward. And not long after the time of these recollections she was to die, quite abruptly and irrelevantly, as the result of the removal of an infected wisdom tooth, with her legend entrusted to various bewildered eyes and hearts and memories she had stamped, including mine, which have sometimes confused her with very dissimilar ladies. She is like Isabel, said my mother in a hushed voice. My grandmother did not admit that this was so. She also admired Isabel but thought her too interfering and was unable to separate her altogether from the excessively close blood-connection with my father, whom I should say, in passage, was a devilish man, possibly not understood but certainly hard to live with . . .

What I saw was not Isabel in my sister but a grown stranger whose beauty sharpened my sense of being alone. I saw that it was all over, put away in a box like a doll no longer cared for, the magical intimacy of our childhood together, the soap-bubble afternoons and the games with paper dolls cut out of dress catalogues and the breathless races here and there on our wheels. For the first time, yes, I saw her beauty. I consciously avowed it to myself, although it seems to me that I turned away from it, averted my look from the pride with which she strolled into the parlor and stood by the mantel mirror to be admired. And it was then, about that time, that I began to find life unsatisfactory as an explanation of itself and was forced to adopt the method of the artist of not explaining but putting the blocks together in some other way that seems more significant to him. Which is a rather fancy way of saying I started writing . . .

My sister also had a separate occupation which was her study of music, at first conducted under my grandmother's instruction but now entrusted to a professional teacher whose name was Miss Aehle, an almost typical spinster, who lived in a small frame house with a porch covered by moonvines and a fence covered by honeysuckle. Her name was pronounced *Ail*-ly. She supported herself and a paralyzed father by giving lessons in violin and piano, neither of which she played very well herself but for which she had great gifts as a teacher. If not great gifts, at least great enthusiasm. She was a true romanticist. She talked so excitedly that she got ahead of herself and looked bewildered and cried out, What was I saying? She was one of the innocents of the world, appreciated only by her pupils and a few persons a generation older than herself. Her pupils nearly always came to adore her, she gave them a feeling that playing little pieces on the piano or scratching out little tunes on a fiddle made up for everything that was ostensibly wrong in a world made by God but disarrayed by the devil. She was religious and ecstatic. She never admitted that anyone of her pupils, even the ones that were unmistakably tone-deaf, were deficient in musical talent. And the few that could perform tolerably well she was certain had genius. She had two real star pupils, my sister, on the piano, and a boy named Richard Miles who studied the violin. Her enthusiasm for these two was unbounded. It is true that my sister had a nice touch and that Richard Miles had a pure tone on the fiddle, but Miss Aehle dreamed of them in terms of playing duets to great ovations in the world's capital cities.

Richard Miles, I think of him now as a boy, for he was about seventeen, but at that time he seemed a complete adult to me, even immeasurably older than my sister who was fourteen. I resented him fiercely even though I began, almost immediately after learning of his existence, to dream about him as I had formerly dreamed of storybook heroes. His name began to inhabit the rectory. It was almost constantly on the lips of my sister, this strange young lady who had come to live with us. It had a curious lightness, that name, in the way that she spoke it. It did not seem to fall from her lips but to be released from them. The moment spoken, it rose into the air and shimmered and floated and took on gorgeous colors the way that soap bubbles did that we used to blow from the sunny back steps in the summer. Those bubbles lifted and floated and they eventually broke but never until other bubbles had floated beside them. Golden they were, and the name of Richard had a golden sound, too. The second name, being Miles, gave a suggestion of distance, so Richard was something both radiant and far away.

My sister's obsession with Richard may have been even more intense than mine. Since mine was copied from hers, it was probably hers that was greater in the beginning. But while mine was of a shy and sorrowful kind, involved with my sense of abandonment, hers at first seemed to be joyous. She had fallen in love. As always, I followed suit. But while love made her brilliant, at first, it made me laggard and dull. It filled me with sad confusion. It tied my tongue or made it stammer and it flashed so unbearably in my eyes that I had to turn them away. These are the intensities that one cannot live with, that he has to outgrow if he wants to survive. But who can help grieving for them? If the blood vessels could hold them, how much better to keep those early loves with us? But if we did, the veins would break and the passion explode into darkness long before the necessary time for it.

I remember one afternoon in fall when my sister and I were walking along a street when Richard Miles appeared suddenly before us from somewhere with a startling cry. I see him bounding, probably down the steps of Miss Aehle's white cottage, emerging unexpectedly from the vines. Probably Miss Aehle's because he bore his violin case, and I remember thinking how closely it resembled a little coffin, a coffin made for a small child or a doll. About people you knew in your childhood it is rarely possible to remember their appearance except as ugly or beautiful or light or dark. Richard was light and he was probably more beautiful than any boy

I have seen since. I do not even remember if he was light in the sense of being blond or if the lightness came from a quality in him deeper than hair or skin. Yes, probably both, for he was one of those people who move in light, provided by practically everything about them. This detail I do remember. He wore a white shirt, and through its cloth could be seen the fair skin of his shoulders. And for the first time, prematurely, I was aware of skin as an attraction. A thing that might be desirable to touch. This awareness entered my mind, my senses, like the sudden streak of flame that follows a comet. And my undoing, already started by Richard's mere coming toward us, was now completed. When he turned to me and held his enormous hand out, I did a thing so grotesque that I could never afterwards be near him without a blistering sense of shame. Instead of taking the hand I ducked away from him. I made a mumbling sound that could have had very little resemblance to speech, and then brushed past their two figures, his and my beaming sister's, and fled into a drugstore just beyond.

That same fall the pupils of Miss Aehle performed in a concert. This concert was held in the parish house of my grandfather's church. And for weeks preceding it the pupils made preparation for the occasion which seemed as important as Christmas. My sister and Richard Miles were to play a duet, she on the piano, of course, and he on the violin. They practiced separately and they practiced together. Separately my sister played the piece very well, but for some reason, more portentous than it seemed at the time, she had great difficulty in playing to

Richard's accompaniment. Suddenly her fingers would turn to thumbs, her wrists would flatten out and become cramped, her whole figure would hunch rigidly toward the piano and her beauty and grace would vanish. It was strange, but Miss Aehle was certain that it would be overcome with repeated practice. And Richard was patient, he was incredibly patient, he seemed to be far more concerned for my sister's sake than his own. Extra hours of practice were necessary. Sometimes when they had left Miss Aehle's, at the arrival of other pupils, they would continue at our house. The afternoons were consequently unsafe. I never knew when the front door might open on Richard's dreadful beauty and his greeting which I could not respond to, could not endure, must fly grotesquely away from. But the house was so arranged that although I hid in my bedroom at these hours of practice, I was still able to watch them at the piano. My bedroom looked out upon the staircase which descended into the parlor where they practiced. The piano was directly within my line of vision. It was in the parlor's lightest corner, with lace-curtained windows on either side of it, the sunlight only fretted by patterns of lace and ferns.

During the final week before the concert — or was it recital they called it? — Richard Miles came over almost invariably at four in the afternoon, which was the last hour of really good sunlight in late October. And always a little before that time I would lower the green blind in my bedroom and with a fantastic stealth, as if a sound would betray a disgusting action, I would open the door two inches, an aperture just enough to enclose the piano corner as by the lateral boundaries of a stage. When I heard them enter the front door, or even before, when I saw their shadows thrown against the oval glass and curtain the door surrounded or heard their voices as they climbed to the porch, I would flatten myself on my belly on the cold floor and remain in that position as long as they stayed, no matter how my knees or elbows ached, and I was so fearful of betraying this watch that I kept over them while they practiced that I hardly dared to breathe.

The transference of my interest to Richard now seemed complete. I would barely notice my sister at the piano, groan at her repeated blunders only in sympathy for him. When I recall what a little puritan I was in those days, there must have been a shocking ambivalence in my thoughts and sensations as I gazed down upon him through the crack of the door. How on earth did I explain to myself, at that time, the fascination of his physical being without, at the same time, confessing to myself that I was a little monster of sensuality? Or was that actually before I had begun to associate the sensual with the impure, an error that tortured me during and after pubescence, or did I, and this seems most likely, now, say to myself, Yes, Tom, you're a monster! But that's how it is and there's nothing to be done about it. And so continued to feast my eyes on his beauty. This much is certain. Whatever resistance there may have been from the "legion of decency" in my soul was exhausted in the first skirmish, not exterminated but thoroughly trounced, and its subsequent complaints were in the form of unseen blushes. Not that there was really anything to be ashamed of in adoring the beauty of

Richard. It was surely made for that purpose, and boys of my age made to be stirred by such ideals of grace. The sheer white cloth in which I had originally seen his upper body was always worn by it, and now, in those afternoons, because of the position of the piano between two windows that cast their beams at cross angles, the white material became diaphanous with light, the torso shone through it, faintly pink and silver, the nipples on the chest and the armpits a little darker, and the diaphragm visibly pulsing as he breathed. It is possible that I have seen more graceful bodies, but I am not sure that I have, and his remains, I believe, a subconscious standard. And looking back upon him now, and upon the devout little mystic of carnality that I was as I crouched on a chill bedroom floor, I think of Camilla Rucellai, that highstrung mystic of Florence who is supposed to have seen Pico della Mirandola entering the streets of that city on a milk-white horse in a storm of sunlight and flowers, and to have fainted at the spectacle of him, and murmured, as she revived, *He will pass in the time of lilies!* meaning that he would die early, since nothing so fair could decline by common degrees in a faded season. The light was certainly there in all its fullness, and even a kind of flowers, at least shadows of them, for there were flowers of lace in the window curtains and actual branches of fern which the light projected across him; no storm of flowers but the shadows of flowers which are perhaps more fitting.

The way that he lifted and handled his violin! First he would roll up the sleeves of his white shirt and remove his necktie and loosen his collar as though he were making preparations for love. Then there was a metallic snap as he released the lock on the case of the violin. Then the upper lid was pushed back and the sunlight fell on the dazzling interior of the case. It was plush-lined and the plush was emerald. The violin itself was somewhat darker than blood and even more lustrous. To Richard I think it must have seemed more precious. His hands and his arms as he lifted it from the case, they said the word love more sweetly than speech could say it, and, oh, what precocious fantasies their grace and tenderness would excite in me. I was a wounded soldier, the youngest of the regiment and he, Richard, was my young officer, jeopardizing his life to lift me from the field where I had fallen and carry me back to safety in the same cradle of arms that supported his violin now. The dreams, perhaps, went further, but I have already dwelt sufficiently upon the sudden triumph of unchastity back of my burning eyes; that needs no more annotation . . .

I now feel some anxiety that this story will seem to be losing itself like a path that has climbed a hill and then lost itself in an overgrowth of brambles. For I have now told you all but one of the things that stand out very clearly, and yet I have not approached any sort of conclusion. There is, of course, a conclusion. However indefinite, there always is some point which serves that need of remembrances and stories.

The remaining very clear thing is the evening of the recital in mid-November, but before an account of that, I should tell more of my sister in this troubled state of hers. It might be possible to willfully thrust myself into her mind, her emotions, but I question the wisdom of it: for at that time I was an almost hostile onlooker where she was concerned. Hurt feelings and jealous feelings were too thickly involved in my view of her at that time. As though she were being punished for a betrayal of our childhood companionship, I felt a gratification tinged with contempt at her difficulties in the duet with Richard. One evening I overhead a telephone call which mother received from Miss Aehle. Miss Aehle was first perplexed and now genuinely alarmed and totally mystified by the sudden decline of my sister's vaunted aptitude for the piano. She had been singing her praises for months. Now it appeared that my sister was about to disgrace her publicly, for she was not only unable, suddenly, to learn new pieces but was forgetting the old ones. It had been planned, originally, for her to play several solo numbers at the recital before and leading up to the duet with Richard. The solos now had to be canceled from the program, and Miss Aehle was even fearful that my sister would not be able to perform in the duet. She wondered if my mother could think of some reason why my sister had undergone this very inopportune and painful decline? Was she sleeping badly, how was her appetite, was she very moody? Mother came away from the telephone in a very cross humor with the teacher. She repeated all the complaints and apprehensions and questions to my grandmother who said nothing but pursed her lips and shook her head while she sewed like one of those venerable women who understand and govern the fates of mortals, but she had nothing to offer in the way of a practical solution except to say that perhaps it was a mistake for brilliant children to be pushed into things like this so early . . .

Richard stayed patient with her most of the time, and there were occasional periods of revival, when she would attack the piano with an explosion of confidence and the melodies would surge beneath her fingers like birds out of cages. Such a resurgence would never last till the end of a piece. There would be a stumble, and then another collapse. Once Richard himself was unstrung. He pushed his violin high into the air like a broom sweeping cobwebs off the ceiling. He strode around the parlor brandishing it like that and uttering groans that were both sincere and comic; when he returned to the piano, where she crouched in dismay, he took hold of her shoulders and gave them a shake. She burst into tears and would have fled upstairs but he caught hold of her by the newel post of the staircase. He would not let go of her. He detained her with murmurs I couldn't quite hear, and drew her gently back to the piano corner. And then he sat down on the piano stool with his great hands gripping each side of her narrow waist while she sobbed with her face averted and her fingers knotting together. And while I watched them from my cave of darkness, my body learned, at least three years too early, the fierceness and fire of the will of life to transcend the single body, and so to continue to follow light's curve and time's . . .

The evening of the recital my sister complained at supper that her hands were stiff, and she kept rubbing them together and even held them over the spout of the

A VIOLIN CASE

teapot to warm them with the steam. She looked very
pretty, I remember, when she was dressed. Her color
was higher than I had ever seen it, but there were tiny
beads of sweat at her temples and she ordered me angrily
out of her room when I appeared in the doorway before
she was ready to pass the family's inspection. She wore
silver slippers and a very grownup-looking dress that
was the greenish sea-color of her eyes. It had the low
waist that was fashionable at that time and there were
silver beads on it in loops and fringes. Her bedroom was
steaming from the adjoining bath. She opened the window. Grandmother slammed it down, declaring that
she would catch cold. Oh, leave me alone, she answered.
The muscles in her throat were curiously prominent as
she stared in the glass. Stop powdering, said my grandmother, you're caking your face with powder. Well, it's
my face, she retorted. And then came near to flying
into a tantrum at some small critical comment offered
by Mother. I have no talent, she said, I have no talent for
music! Why do I have to do it, why do you make me,
why was I forced into this? Even my grandmother
finally gave up and retired from the room. But when it
came time to leave for the parish house, my sister came
downstairs looking fairly collected and said not another
word as we made our departure. Once in the automobile
she whispered something about her hair being mussed.
She kept her stiff hands knotted in her lap. We drove
first to Miss Aehle's and found her in a state of hysteria
because Richard had fallen off a bicycle that afternoon
and skinned his fingers. She was sure it would hinder
his playing. But when we arrived at the parish house,

98

Richard was already there as calm as a duckpond, playing delicately with the mute on the strings and no apparent disability. We left them, teacher and performers, in the cloakroom and went to take our seats in the auditorium which was beginning to fill, and I remember noticing a half-erased inscription on a blackboard which had something to do with a Sunday School lesson.

No, it did not go off well. They played without sheet music, and my sister made all the mistakes she had made in practicing and several new ones. She could not seem to remember the composition beyond the first few pages; it was a fairly long one, and those pages she repeated twice, possibly even three times. But Richard was heroic. He seemed to anticipate every wrong note that she struck and to bring down his bow on the strings with an extra strength to cover and rectify it. When she began to lose control altogether, I saw him edging up closer to her position, so that his radiant figure shielded her partly from view, and I saw him, at a crucial moment, when it seemed that the duet might collapse altogether, raise his bow high in the air, at the same time catching his breath in a sort of "Hah!" a sound I heard much later from bullfighters daring a charge, and lower it to the strings in a masterful sweep that took the lead from my sister and plunged them into the passage that she had forgotten in her panic. . . . For a bar or two, I think, she stopped playing, sat there motionless, stunned. And then, finally, when he turned his back to the audience and murmured something to her, she started again. She started playing again but Richard played so brilliantly and so richly that the piano was barely noticeable underneath him. And so they got through it, and when it was finished they received an ovation. My sister started to rush for the cloakroom. But Richard seized her wrist and held her back. Then something odd happened. Instead of bowing she suddenly turned and pressed her forehead against him, pressed it against the lapel of his blue serge suit. He blushed and bowed and touched her waist with his fingers, gently, his eyes glancing down . . .

We drove home in silence, almost. There was a conspiracy to ignore that anything unfortunate had happened. My sister said nothing. She sat with her hands knotted in her lap exactly as she had been before the recital, and when I looked at her I noticed that her shoulders were too narrow and her mouth a little too wide for real beauty, and that her recent habit of hunching made her seem a little bit like an old lady being imitated by a child.

At that point Richard Miles faded out of our lives for my sister refused to continue to study music, and not long afterwards my father received an advancement, an office job as a minor executive in a northern shoe company, and we moved from the South. No, I am not putting all of these things in their exact chronological order, I may as well confess it, but if I did I would violate my honor as a teller of stories . . .

As for Richard, the truth is exactly congruous to the poem. A year or so later we learned, in that northern city to which we had moved, that he had died of pneumonia. And then I remembered the case of his violin, and how it resembled so much a little black coffin made for a child or a doll . . .

HARD CANDY

HARD CANDY

ONCE upon a time in a southern seaport of America there was a seventy-year-old retired merchant named Mr. Krupper, a man of gross and unattractive appearance and with no close family connections. He had been the owner of a small sweetshop, which he had sold out years before to a distant and much younger cousin with whose parents, no longer living, he had emigrated to America fifty-some years ago. But Mr. Krupper had not altogether relinquished his hold on the shop and this was a matter of grave dissatisfaction to the distant cousin and his wife and their twelve-year-old daughter, whom Mr. Krupper, with an old man's interminable affection for a worn-out joke, still invariably addressed and referred to as "The Complete Little Citizen of the World," a title invented for her by the cousin himself when she was a child of five and when her trend to obesity was not so serious a matter as it now appeared. Now it sounded like a malicious jibe to the cousins, although Mr. Krupper always said it with a benevolent air, "How is the complete little citizen of the world today?" as he gave her a quick little pat on the cheek or the shoulder, and the child would answer, "Drop dead!" which the old man never heard, for his high blood pressure gave him a continual singing in the ears which drowned out all remarks that were not shouted at him. At least he seemed not to hear it, but one could not be sure about Mr. Krupper. The degree of his simplicity was hard to determine.

Sick old people live at varying distances from the world. Sometimes they seem to be a thousand miles out on some invisible sea with the sails set in an opposite direction, and nothing on shore seems to reach them, but then, at another time, the slightest gesture or faintest whisper will reach them. But dislike and even hatred seems to be something to which they develop a lack of sensibility with age. It seems to come as naturally as the coarsening of the skin itself. And Mr. Krupper showed no sign of being aware of how deeply his cousins detested his morning calls at the shop. The family of three would retire to the rooms behind the shop when they saw him coming, unless they happened to be detained by customers, but the old man would wait patiently until one of them was forced to reappear. "Don't hurry, I have got nothing but time," he used to say. He never left without scooping up a fistful of hard candies which he kept in a paper bag in his pocket. This was the little custom which the cousins found most exasperating of all, but they could do nothing about it.

It was this way: the little shop had maintained itself so poorly since the cousins took over that they had never been able to produce more than the interest on the final payment that was due to Mr. Krupper. So they were forced to permit his depredations. Once the cousin, the male one, sourly remarked that Mr. Krupper must have a very fine set of teeth for a man of his years if he could eat so much hard candy, and the old man had replied that he didn't eat it himself. "Who does?" inquired the cousin, and the old man said, with a yellow-toothed grin, "The birds!" The cousins had never seen the old man eat a piece of the candy. Sometimes it accumulated in the paper bag till it swelled out of his pocket like a great tumor, and then other times it would be mysteriously depleted, flattened out, barely visible under the shiny blue flap of the pocket, and then the cousin would say to his wife or daughter, "It looks like the birds were hungry." These ominous and angry little jests had been continuing almost without variation over a very long time. The magnitude of the cousins' dislike for the old man was as difficult to determine as the degree of the old man's insensibility to it. After all, it was based on nothing important, two or three cents' worth of hard candies a day and a few little apparently innocent exchanges of words among them, but it had been going on so long, for so many years. The cousins were not imaginative people, not even sufficiently so to complain to themselves about the tepid and colorless regularity of their lives and the heartbreaking fruitlessness of their dull will to go on and do well and keep going, and the little girl blowing up like a rubber toy, continually, senselessly and sadly popping the sweets in her mouth, not even knowing that she was doing it, crying sadly when told that she had to stop it, insisting quite truthfully that she didn't know she had done it, and five minutes later, doing it again, getting her fat hands slapped and crying again but not remembering later, already fatter than either of her fat parents and developing gross, unladylike habits, such as belching and waiting on customers with a running nose and being called Fatty at school and coming home crying about it. All of these things could easily be associated in some way with the inescapable morning calls of old Mr. Krupper, and all of these little sorrows and resentments could conveniently adopt the old man as their incarnate image, which they did . . .

In the course of this story, and very soon now, it will be necessary to make some disclosures about Mr. Krupper of a nature too coarse to be dealt with very directly in a work of such brevity. The grossly naturalistic details of a life, contained in the enormously wide context of that life, are softened and qualified by it, but when you attempt to set those details down in a tale, some measure of obscurity or indirection is called for to provide the same, or even approximate, softening effect that existence in time gives to those gross elements in the life itself. When I say that there was a certain mystery in the life of Mr. Krupper, I am beginning to approach those things in the only way possible without a head-on violence that would disgust and destroy and which would actually falsify the story.

To have hatred and contempt for a person, as the cousins had for old Mr. Krupper, calls for the assumption that you know practically everything of any significance about him. If you admit that he is a mystery, you admit that the hostility may be unjust. So the cousins failed to see anything mysterious about the old man and his existence. Sometimes the male cousin or his wife would follow him to the door when he went out of the shop, they would stand at the door and stare after him as he shuffled along the block, usually with one hand clasped over the pocket containing the bag of hard candies as if it were a bird that might spring out again, but it was not curiosity about him, it was not interested speculation concerning the old man's goings and comings that motivated their stares at his departing back, it was only the sort of look that you turn to give a rock on which you have stubbed your toe, a senselessly vicious look turned upon an insensibly malign object. There was not room in the doorway for both of the grown cousins, fat as they were, to stare after him at once. The one that got there first was the one that stared after him and the one that uttered the "faugh" of disgust as he finally disappeared from view, a "faugh" as disgusted as if they had penetrated to the very core of those mysteries about him which we are approaching by cautious indirection. The other one of the cousins, the one that had failed to achieve first place at the door, would be standing close behind but with a blocked vision, and the old man's progress down the street and his eventual turning would be a vicarious spectacle enjoyed, or rather detested, only through the commentary provided by the cousin in the favored position. Naturally there was not much to comment upon. An old man's progress down a city block is not eventful. Sometimes the one in the door would say, *He has picked up something on the sidewalk.* The other one would answer, *Faugh! What?* — momentarily alarmed that it might have been something of value, gratified to learn that the old man had dropped it again some paces beyond. Or the reporter would say, *He is looking into a window! Which one? The haberdashery window! Faugh! He'll never buy nothing . . .* But the comments would always end with the announcement that he had crossed the street to the small public square in which Mr. Krupper seemed to spend all his mornings after the call at the sweetshop. The comments and the stares and the faughs of disgust betrayed no real interest or curiosity or speculation about him, only the fiercely senseless attention given to something acknowledged to have no mysteries whatsoever . . .

For that matter, it would be hard for anybody to discover, from outside observation not carried to the point of actual sleuthing, what it was that gave Mr. Krupper the certain air he had of being engaged in something far more momentous than the ordinary meanderings of an old man retired from business and without close family ties. To notice something you would have to be looking for something, and even then a morning might pass or part of an afternoon or even sometimes a whole day without anything meeting your observation that would strike you as a notable difference. Yes, he was like almost any other old man of the sort that you see stooping painfully over to collect the scattering pages of an abandoned

newspaper or shuffling out of a public lavatory with
fingers fumbling at buttons or loitering upon a corner
as if for a while undecided which way to turn. Unat-
tached and aimless, these old men are always infatuated
with little certainties and regularities such as those that
ordered the life of Mr. Krupper as seen from outside.
Habit is living. Anything unexpected reminds them of
death. They will stand for half an hour staring fiercely
at an occupied bench rather than take one which is
empty but which is not familiar and therefore seems
insecure to them, the sort of a cold bench on which
the heart might flutter and stop or the bowels suddenly
loosen a hot flow of blood. These old men are always
picking little things up and are very hesitant about putting anything down, even if it is something quite worth-
less which they had picked up only a moment before out
of simple lack of attention. They usually have on a hat,
and in the South, it is usually a very old white one turned
yellow as their teeth or gray as their cracked fingernails
and stubbly beards. And they have a way of removing
this hat now and then with a gesture that looks like a
deferential salute, as if some great invisible lady had
passed before them and given them a slight bow of recognition; and then, a few moments later, when the faint
breeze has tickled and tousled their scalps a bit, the hat
goes back on, more slowly and carefully than it had been
removed; and then they gently change their position
on the bench, always first curving their fingers tenderly
under the ransacked home of their gender. Sighs and
grunts are their language with themselves, speaking always of a weariness and a dull confusion, either allevi-

ated by some little change or momentarily aggravated by it. Ordinarily there is no more mystery in their lives than there is in a gray dollar-watch which is almost consumed by the moments that it has ticked off. They are the nice old men, the sweet old men and the clean old men of the world. But our old man, Mr. Krupper, is a bird of a different feather, and it is now time, in fact it is probably already past time, to follow him further than the public square into which he turned when the cousins no longer could watch him. It is necessary to advance the hour of the day, to skip past the morning and the early afternoon, spent in the public square and the streets of that vicinity, and it is necessary to follow Mr. Krupper by streetcar into another section of the city.

No sooner has he got upon this streetcar than Mr. Krupper undergoes a certain alteration, not too subtle to betray some outward signals: for he sits in the streetcar with an air of alertness that he did not have on the bench in the public square, he sits more erect and his various little gestures, fishing in his pocket for something, shifting about on the dirty blond straw bench, changing the level of the window shade, are all executed with greater liveliness and precision, as if they were the motions of a much younger man. Anticipation does that, and we would notice that about him, that mysterious attitude of expectancy, very slightly but noticeably increasing as the car whines along to the other part of the city. And we might even notice him beginning to color faintly as he prepares to ring the bell and rise from his seat a block in advance of the stop at which he descends. When he descends it is with all the painful, wheezing concentration of an inexpert climber following a rope down the side of an Alp, and his muttered *thanks* is too low to be audible as he sets foot to pavement. This he does, finally, with a vast sigh, an almost cosmic respiration, and he lifts his eyes well above the level of the roof-tops without appearing to look into the sky, a purely mechanical elevation that might once have had meaning, a salute to rational Providence which is supposed to be situated somewhere above the level of the roof-tops, if anywhere at all. And now Mr. Krupper has arrived within a block of where he is actually going and which is the place where the mysteries of his nature are to be made unpleasantly manifest to us. For some reason, a silly, squeamish kind of dissimulation, Mr. Krupper prefers to walk the last block to his destination rather than descend from the streetcar immediately before it. As he walks, and still a little before we know where he is going, we notice him making various anxious little preparations and adjustments. First he pats the bag of hard candies. Then he reaches into the opposite pocket of his jacket and pulls out a handful of quarters, counts them, makes sure there are exactly eight, and drops them back in the pocket. He then removes from the breast pocket of the jacket, from behind a protruding white handkerchief, always the whitest thing in his possession, a pair of dark-lensed glasses, lenses so dark that the eyes are not visible behind them. He puts these on. And now for the first time he seemingly dares to look directly toward the place that attracts him, and if we follow his glance we see that it is nothing less apparently innocent than an old theater building called the Joy Rio.

So that much of the mystery is dissolved, and it is nothing more ostensibly remarkable than the little clock-like regularity of going three times a week, on Monday, Thursday and Saturday afternoons at about half-past four, to a certain third-rate cinema situated near the water front and known as the Joy Rio. And if we followed Mr. Krupper only as far as the door of that cinema, nothing of an esoteric nature would be noticeable, unless you thought it peculiar that he should go three times a week to a program changed only on Mondays or that he never paused to inspect the outside posters in that gradual, reflective manner of most old men who make a habit of going to the movies but went directly up to the ticket window, or that even before he crossed the street to the block on which the cinema was located, he not only put on the secretive-looking glasses but accelerated his pace as if he were urged along by a bitter wind that nipped particularly at the back of the old man's neck. But naturally we are not going to follow him only that far, we are going to follow him past the ticket window and into the interior of the theater. And right away, as soon as we have made that entrance, a premonition of something out of the ordinary is forced upon us. For the Joy Rio is not, by any means, an ordinary theater. It is the ghost of a once elegant house where plays and operas were performed long ago. But the building does not exist within the geographic limits of that part of the city which is regarded as having an historical value. Its decline into squalor, its conversion into a third-rate cinema, has not been particularly annotated by a sentimental press or public. Actually it is only when the lights are brought on, for a brief interval between shows or at their conclusion, that the place is distinguishable from any other cheap movie-house. And then it is only distinguishable by looking upwards. Looking upwards you see that it contains not only the usual orchestra and balcony sections but two tiers of boxes extending in horseshoe design from one side of the proscenium to the other, but the faded gilt, the terribly abused red damask of these upper reaches of the Joy Rio never bloom into sufficient light to make a strong impression from the downstairs. You have to follow Mr. Krupper up the great marble staircase that still rises beyond the balcony level before you really begin to explore the physical mysteries of the place. And that, of course, is what we are going to do.

That is what we are going to do, but first we are going to orientate ourselves a little more specifically in time, for although these visits of Mr. Krupper to the Joy Rio are events of almost timeless repetition, our story is the narrative of one particular time and involving another individual, both of which must first be established, together, before we resume the company of Mr. Krupper.

We come, then, to a certain afternoon when a shadowy youth who may as well remain nameless has come into the Joy Rio without any knowledge of its peculiar character and for no other reason than to catch a few hours' sleep, for he is a stranger in the city who does not have the price of a hotel bedroom and who is in terror of being picked up for vagrancy and set to work for the city at no pay and a poor diet. He is very sleepy, so sleepy that his motions are more instinctive than conscious. The film showing that afternoon at the Joy Rio is an epic of the western ranges, full of loud voices and gunplay, so the boy turns as far away from the noisy and brilliant screen as the geography of the Joy Rio will allow him. He climbs the stairs to the first gallery. It is dark up there, but still noisy; so he continues his ascent, only faintly surprised to find that it is possible to do so. The darkness increases as he approaches the second level and the clamor of the screen is more than correspondingly reduced. In the gloom, as he makes a turn of the stairs, he passes what seems for a moment to be, almost believably, a naked female figure. He pauses there long enough to find out that it is only a piece of life-size statuary, cold to the fingers, and disappointingly hard in the places where he fondly touches it, a nymph made of cobwebbed stone in a niche at the turn of the stairs. He goes on up, and sleep is already descending on him, a black, fuzzy blanket, by the time he has wandered blindly into that one of the row of boxes which is to be occupied also, in a few minutes, by the old man whose mysteries are the sad ones of the Joy Rio . . .

By the time that Mr. Krupper arrives at the box and assures the usher's neutrality with a liberal tip, the boy has plummeted like a stone to the depths of sleep, all the way down to the velvety bottom of it, without a ripple to mark where he has fallen. Head lolls forward and thighs move apart and fingers almost brush the floor. The wet lips have fallen apart and the breath whistles faintly but not enough to be heard by Mr. Krupper. It is so dim in the box that the fat old man nearly sits down in the boy's lap before he discovers that his usual seat has been taken. At first Mr. Krupper thinks this nearly invisible companion may be a certain Italian youth of his acquaintance who sometimes shares the box with him for a few minutes, at rare intervals, five or six weeks apart, and he whispers inquiringly the name of this youth, which is Bruno, but he gets no answer, and he decides, no, it could not be Bruno. The slight odor that made him think it might be, an odor made up of sweat and tobacco and the prodigality of certain youthful glands, is not at all unfamiliar to the old man's nose, and while he is now convinced that it is not Bruno, this time, it nevertheless makes him feel a stir of anticipatory happiness in his bosom, which also heaves from the exertion of having just climbed two flights of the grand staircase. In a crouched position he locates the other chair and carefully sets it where he wants it to be, at a nicely calculated space from the one that is occupied by the sleeper, and then Mr. Krupper deposits himself on the seat with the stiff-kneed elaboration of an old camel. It sets the blood charging through him at breakneck speed. Ah, well. That much is completed.

A few minutes pass in which Mr. Krupper's eyesight adjusts itself to the almost pitch-black condition of light in the box, but even then it is impossible to make out the figure beside him in any detail. Yes, it is young, it is slender. The hair is dark and lustrous, the odor is captivating. But the head of the sleeper has lolled a bit to one side, the side away from Mr. Krupper, and sometimes it is possible, in the dark, to make very dangerous mistakes. There are certain pursuits in which even the most cautious man must depart from absolute caution if he intends at all to enjoy them. Mr. Krupper knew that. He had known it for a great many years, and that was why he had observed such elaborate caution in nearly every other department of his life, to compensate for those necessary breaches of caution that were the sad concomitant of his kind of pleasure. And so as a measure of caution, Mr. Krupper digs into his pocket for a box of matches which he carries with him only for this purpose, to secure that one relatively clear glance at a fellow-occupant of the dark box. He strikes the match and leans a little bit forward. And then his heart, aged seventy and already strained from the recent exertion of the stairs, undergoes an alarming spasm, for never in this secret life of his, never in thirty years' attendance of matinees at the Joy Rio, has old Mr. Krupper discovered beside him, even now within contact, inspiring the dark with its warm animal fragrance, any dark youth of remotely equivalent beauty.

The match burns his fingers, he lets it fall to the floor. His vest is half unbuttoned, but he unbuttons it further to draw a deep breath. Something is hurting in him, first in his chest, then lower, a nervous contraction of his unhealthy intestines. He whispers to himself the German word for calmness. He leans back in the uncomfortable small chair and attempts to look at the faraway flickering square of the motion picture. The excitement in his body will not subside. The respiration will not stabilize. The contraction of his intestinal nerves and muscles gives him sharp pain, and he is wondering, for a moment, if it will not be necessary for him to return hastily downstairs to move his bowels. But then, all at once, the sleeper beside him stirs and half sits up in the gloom. The lolling head suddenly jerks erect and cries a sharp word in Spanish. "Excuse me," says Mr. Krupper, softly, involuntarily. "I didn't know you were there." The youth gives a grunting laugh and seems to relax once more. He makes a sad, sighing sound as he slouches down once more in the chair beside Mr. Krupper. Mr. Krupper feels somewhat calmer now. It is hard to say why but the almost unbearable acuteness of the proximity, the discovery, now has passed, and Mr. Krupper himself assumes a more relaxed position in his hard chair. The muscular spasm and the tachycardia now are gently eased off and the bowels appear to be settled. Minutes pass in the box. Mr. Krupper has the impression that the youth beside him, that vision, has not yet returned to slumber, although the head has lolled again to one side, this time the side that is toward him, and the limbs fallen apart with the former relaxation. Slowly, as if secretively, Mr. Krupper digs in his jacket pocket for the hard candies. One he unwraps and places in his own mouth which is burning and dry. Then he extracts another which he extends on the palm of his hand, which shakes a little, toward the youthful stranger. He clears his throat which feels as if it would be difficult to produce a sound, and manages to say, "A piece of candy?" "Huh," says the youth. The syllable has the sound of being startled. For a moment it seems that he is bewildered or angry. He make no immediate move to take or reject the candy, he only sits up and stares. Then all at once he grunts. His fingers snatch at the candy and pop it directly into his mouth, paper wrapping and all. Mr. Krupper hastens to warn him that the candy is wrapped up. He grunts again and removes it from his mouth, and Mr. Krupper hears him plucking the rather brittle wrapping-paper away, and afterwards he hears the candy crunching noisily between the jaws of the youth. Before the jaws have stopped crunching, Mr. Krupper has dug the whole bag out of his pocket and now he says, "Take some more, take several pieces, there's lots." Again the youth hesitates slightly. Again he grunts. Then he digs his hand into the bag and Mr. Krupper feels it lighter by half when the hand has been removed. "Hungry?" he whispers with a questioning note. The youth grunts again, affirmatively and in a way that seems friendly. Don't hurry, thinks Mr. Krupper. Don't hurry, there's plenty of time, he's not going to go up in smoke like the dream that he looks! So he puts the remains of the candy in his pocket, and makes a low humming sound as of gratification as he looks back toward the flickering screen where the cowboy hero is galloping into a sunset. In a moment the picture will end and the lights will go up for an interval of a minute before the program commences all over again. There is, of course, some danger that the youth will leave. That possibility has got to be considered, but the affirmative answer to the question "Hungry?" has already given some basis, not quite a pledge, of continuing association between them.

Now just before the lights go up, Mr. Krupper makes a bold move. He reaches into the pocket opposite to the one containing the bag of hard candy and scoops out all that remain of the quarters, about six altogether, and jostles them ever so slightly together in his fist so they tinkle a bit. This is all that he does. And the lights come gradually on, like daybreak only a little accelerated; the once elegant theater blooms dully as a winter rose beneath him as he leans forward in order to seem to be interested in the downstairs. He is a little panicky but he knows that the period of light will be very short, not more than a minute or two. But he also knows that he is fat and ugly. Mr. Krupper knows that he is a terrible old man, shameful and despicable even to those who tolerate his caresses, perhaps even more so to those than to the others who only see him. He does not deceive himself at all about that, and that is why he took the six quarters out and shook them together a little before the lights were brought on. Yes, now. Now the lights are beginning to darken again, and the youth is still there. If he is now alert to the unpleasant character of Mr. Krupper's appearance, he is nevertheless still beside him. And he is still unwrapping the bits of hard candy and crunching them between his powerful young jaws, steadily, with the automatic, invariable rhythm of a horse masticating his food.

The lights are now down again and the panic has passed. Mr. Krupper abandons the pretense of staring downstairs and leans back once more in the unsteady chair. Now something rises in him, something heroic, determined, and he leans toward the youth, turning around a little, and with his left hand he finds the right hand of the youth and offers the coins. At first the hand of the youth will not change its position, will not respond to the human and metallic pressure. Mr. Krupper is about to fly once more into panic, but then, at the very moment when his hand is about to withdraw from contact with the hand of the youth, that hand turns about, revolves to bring the palm upward. The coins descend, softly, with a slight tinkle, and Mr. Krupper knows that the contract is sealed between them.

WHEN around midnight the lights of the Joy Rio were brought up for the last time that evening, the body of Mr. Krupper was discovered in his remote box of the theater with his knees on the floor and his ponderous torso wedged between two wobbly gilt chairs as if he had expired in an attitude of prayer. The notice of the old man's death was given unusual prominence for the obituary of someone who had no public character and whose private character was so peculiarly low. But evidently the private character of Mr. Krupper was to remain anonymous in the memories of those anonymous persons who had enjoyed or profited from his company in the tiny box at the Joy Rio, for the notice contained no mention of anything of such a special nature. It was composed by a spinsterly reporter who had been impressed by the sentimental values of a seventy-year-old retired merchant dying of thrombosis at a cowboy thriller with a split bag of hard candies in his pocket and the floor about him littered with sticky wrappers, some of which even adhered to the shoulders and sleeves of his jacket.

It was, among the cousins, the Complete Little Citizen of the World who first caught sight of this astonishingly agreeable item in the paper and who announced the tidings in a voice as shrill as a steam whistle announcing the meridian of the day, and it was she that exclaimed hours later, while the little family was still boiling with the excitement and glory of it, *Just think, Papa, the old man choked to death on our hard candy!*

RUBIO Y MORENA

RUBIO
Y MORENA

THE writer Kamrowski had many acquaintances, especially now that his name had begun to acquire some public luster, and he also had a few friends which he had kept over the years the way that you keep a few books you have read several times but are still not willing to part with. He was essentially a lonely man, not self-sufficient but living as though he were. He had never been able to believe that anybody sincerely cared much about him and perhaps no one did. When women treated him tenderly, which sometimes happened in spite of his reserve, he suspected them of trying to pull the wool over his eyes. He was not at ease with them. It even embarrassed him to sit across from a woman at a restaurant table. He could not return her look across the table nor keep his mind on the bright things she was saying. If she happened to wear an ornament at her throat or on the lapel of her jacket, he would keep his eyes on this pin and stare at it so intently that finally she would interrupt her talk to ask him why he found it so fascinating or might even unfasten it from her dress and hand it across the table for closer inspection. When going to bed with a woman, desire would often desert his body as soon as he put off his clothes and exposed his nakedness to her. He felt her eyes on him, watching, knowing, involving, and the desire ran out of him like water, leaving him motionless as a dead body on the bed beside her, impervious to her caresses and burning with shame, repulsing her almost roughly if she persisted in trying to waken his passion. But when she had given up trying, when she had finally turned away from his unresponsive body and fallen asleep, then he would turn slowly, warm with desire, not shame, and begin to approach the woman until with a moan of longing, greater than even his fear of her had been, he would rouse her from sleep with the brutal haste of a bull in loveless coupling.

It was not the kind of lovemaking that women respond to with much understanding. There was no tenderness in it, neither before nor after the act was completed, with the frigid embarrassment first and the satiety afterwards, both making him rough and coarse and nearly speechless. He thought of himself as being no good with women, and for that reason his relations with them had been infrequent and fleeting. It was a kind of psychic impotence of which he was bitterly ashamed. He felt it could not be explained, so he never tried to explain it.

RUBIO Y MORENA

And so he was lonely and unsatisfied outside of his work.
He was uniformly kind to everybody just because he
found it easier to be that way, but he forgot nearly all of
his social engagements, or if he happened to remember
one while he was working, he would sigh, not very
deeply, and go on working without even stopping to
call on the phone and say, Excuse me, I'm working. His
attachment to his work was really somewhat absurd,
for he was not an especially good writer. In fact, he was
nearly as awkward in his writing as he had been in his
relations with women. He wrote the way that he had
always made love, with a feeling of apprehension, rushing through it blindly and feverishly as if he were fearful of being unable to complete the act.

You may be wondering why you are presented with
these unpleasantly clinical details in advance of the
story. It is in order to make more understandable the
relationship which the story deals with, a rather singu-
lar relationship between the writer Kamrowski and a
Mexican girl, Amada, which began in the Mexican border town of Laredo, one summer during the war when
Kamrowski was returning from a trip through the
Mexican interior.

Because of his suspiciously foreign name and appearance and a nervous habit of speech that easily gave the
impression of an accent, Kamrowski had been detained
at the border by customs and immigration officials. They
had confiscated his papers for an examination by experts
in code, and Kamrowski had been forced to remain in
Laredo while this examination was in progress. He had
taken a room at the Texas Star Hotel. It was intensely

hot, the night he spent there. He lay on the huge sagging deck of the bed and smoked cigarettes. Because it was such a hot night, he lay there naked with the windows open and the door open, too, hoping to make a draft of air on his body. The room was quite dark except for his cigarette and the corridor of the hotel was almost light-less. About three A.M. a figure appeared in the doorway. It was so tall that he took it to be a man. He said nothing but went on smoking and the figure in the doorway appeared to be staring at him. He had heard things about the deportment of guests at the Texas Star Hotel and so he was not surprised when the door pushed farther open and the figure came in and advanced to the edge of the bed. It was only when the head inclined over him and the heavy black hair came tumbling over his bare flesh that he realized the figure to be a woman's. No, he said, but the caller paid no attention and, after a while, Kam-rowski was reconciled to it. Then pleased and, at last, de-lighted. The meeting had been so successful that in the morning Kamrowski had kept her with him. He asked her no questions. She asked him none. They simply went off together, and seemingly it did not matter where they went ...

For a few months Kamrowski and the Mexican girl named Amada had traveled around the southern states in a rattletrap car held together by spit and a prayer, and most of that time the girl sat mutely beside him while he thought his own thoughts. What her thoughts were he had not the least idea and not much concern. He only saw her turn her head once and that was when they were passing down the main street of a little town in

Louisiana. He turned to see what she looked at. A gaudily dressed Negro girl stood on a streetcorner in a cluster
of roughly dressed white men. Amada smiled faintly
and nodded. *Puta*, she said, only that; but the faint
smile of recognition remained on her face for quite a
while after the corner had slipped out of sight. She did
not often smile and that was why the occurrence had
stuck in his mind.

Companionship was not a familiar or easy thing for
Kamrowski, not even the companionship of men. The
girl was the first he had lived with at all continuously,
and to his content he found it possible to forget her presence except as some almost abstract comfort like that of
warmth or of sleep. Sometimes he would feel a little
astonished, a little incredulous over this sudden alliance
of theirs, this accidental coming together of their two so
different lives. Sometimes he wondered just why he had
taken her with him and he could not explain this thing
to himself and yet he did not regret it. He had not realized, at first, what a curious-looking person she was, not
until other people had noticed it for him. Sometimes
when they stopped at a filling station or entered a restaurant at night, he would notice the way strangers looked
at her with a sort of amused surprise, and then he would
look at her too, and he, too, would be amused and surprised at the strangeness of her appearance. She was tall
and narrow-shouldered and most of the flesh of her body
was centered about the hips which were as large as the
rump of a horse. Her hands were large as a man's but
not capable. Their movements were too nervous and
her feet clopped awkwardly around. She was forever

stumbling or getting caught on something because of her ungainly size and motions. Once the sleeve of her jacket got caught in the slammed car door, and instead of quietly opening the door and disengaging the caught sleeve, she began to utter short, whimpering cries and to tug at the caught sleeve till the material gave way and a piece of sleeve tore loose. Afterwards he noticed that her whole body was shaking as if she had just passed through some nervous ordeal and throughout their supper at the hotel café she would keep lifting up the torn sleeve and frowning at it with a mystified expression as if she did not understand how it got that way, then glancing at him with her head slightly tilted in a look of inquiry as if to ask him if he understood what had happened to the torn sleeve. After the supper, when they had gone upstairs, she took out a pair of scissors and cut the sleeve neatly across to give it an edge. He pointed out to her that this made a disparity between the lengths of the two sleeves. Ha ha, said the girl. She held the jacket up to the light. She saw the disparity herself and began to laugh at it. Finally she threw the jacket into the wastepaper basket and she lay down on the bed with a copy of a movie magazine. She thumbed through it rapidly till she came to a picture of a young male star on a beach. She stopped at that page. She drew the magazine close to her eyes and stared at it with her large mouth hanging open for half an hour, while Kamrowski lay on the bed beside her, only comfortably, warmly half-conscious of her until before sleep, as peacefully as he would sleep, he turned to embrace her.

Kamrowski had grown to love her. Unfortunately,

he was even less articulate in speaking about such things than he would have been in trying to write about them. He could not make the girl understand the tenderness he felt toward her. He was not a man who could even say, I love you. The words would not come off his tongue, not even in the intimacies of the night. He could only speak with his body and his hands. With her childlike mind, the girl must have found him altogether baffling. She could not have been able to believe that he loved her, but she must have been equally unable to fathom his reason for staying with her if he did not. Kamrowski would never know how she explained these things to herself or if she tried to explain them or if she was really as mindless as she had seemed — not looking for reasons for things but only accepting that which happens to be as simply being. No. He would never know how. The dark figure in the doorway of the hotel, even mistaken at first for that of a man, did not come into the light. It remained in shadow. *Morena.* She called him *Rubio* sometimes when she touched him. *Rubio* meant blond one. Sometimes he would answer *Morena* which means dark. *Morena.* That's all she was. Something dark. Dark of skin, dark of hair, dark of eyes. But mystery can be loved as well as knowledge and there could be little doubt that Kamrowski loved her.

Nevertheless, a change became evident after they had lived together for less than a year, which may not seem a long time but was actually a relationship of unprecedented duration in the life of Kamrowski. This change seemed to have several reasons, but perhaps the real one was none of those apparent. For one thing, the presence of women had ceased to disturb him so greatly. That nervous block described in the beginning was now so thoroughly dissolved by virtue of the effortless association with Amada, that his libido had now begun to ask for an extended field of play. The mind of a woman no longer emasculated him. The simple half-Indian girl had restored his male dominance. In his heart he knew this and was grateful, but one does not always return a gift with an outward show of devoir. He paid her back very badly. That winter season, which they spent in a southern city, he began to go out in society for the first time in his life, for he had lately become what is called a Name and received a good deal of attention. It was possible, now, to ignore the ornament at the throat of the woman and return, at least now and again, the look of her eyes without too much mortification. It was also possible to make amatory advances before she had gone to sleep.

That winter Kamrowski began to form other attachments of more than a night's duration, one in particular with a young woman who was also a writer and a member of the urban intelligentsia. She had, also, one defect. She wore contact lenses which she used to remove before going to bed and Kamrowski had to ask her not to put them on the table beside the bed but in the little drawer of the table. But this was an unimportant item in the affair which went along smoothly. He began to make love to this girl, Ida, more regularly than he made love to Amada. Now when Amada would turn to him on the bed, he would often avert himself from her and pretend to be sleeping. He would hear her beginning to cry beside him. Her hand would move inquiringly down his body, and once he seized her hand and slammed it roughly away from him. Then she got out of bed. He got up, too, and went into the kitchen and sat there with a pitcher of ice water. He heard her packing her things as she had done often before. Her trunk was a military locker. The bottom of it was filled with random keepsakes, such as restaurant menus, pictures of actors torn from movie magazines, postcards from all the places they had visited in their travels. Sometimes, while she was packing, she would stalk into the kitchen, holding up some article, such as a towel that she had filched from a hotel bathroom. Is this yours or mine? she would ask. He would shrug. She would make a terrible face at him and return to the bedroom to continue her packing. He knew that she would unpack everything in the morning. In the morning she would restore the souvenir menus and postcards to their places about the mirror and the mantel because without him there was no place for her to go and no one to go with. He did not want to feel sorry for her. He was enjoying himself too much to allow a shadow of contrition to weigh upon him too heavily, and so he would think to himself, for self-exoneration, during such scenes: She was only a whore in a third-class hotel where I found her. Why isn't she happy? Well, I don't give a damn!

And yet he was very glad, when he had finished drinking the pitcher of ice water, to find that she was no longer packing but had gone back to bed. Then he would make love to her more tenderly than he had for many weeks past.

It was a morning after an incident such as this that Kamrowski first discovered that the girl had begun to steal from him. Thereafter, whenever he put on his clothes in the morning, he would find his pockets lighter of money than they had been before. At first she took only silver, but as the earnings of his novel increased, she began to increase the amounts of her thefts, taking one dollar bills, then five and ten dollar bills. Finally, Kamrowski had to accuse her of it. She wailed miserably but she did not deny it. For about a week the practice was suspended. Then it started again, first with the silver, increasing again to bills of larger denomination. He tried to thwart her by taking the money out of his pockets and hiding it somewhere about the apartment. But when he did this, she would waken him in the night by her slow and systematic search for it. What are you looking for? he would ask the girl. I am looking for matches, she'd tell him. So at last he humored her in it. He only cashed small checks and let her steal what she wanted. It remained a mystery to him what she did with the money. She apparently bought nothing with it and yet it did not seem to linger in her possession. What did she want with it? She had everything that she needed or seemed to wish. Perhaps it was simply her way of paying him back for the infidelities which he was now practicing all the time.

It was later that winter of their residence in the large southern city that the ill health of Amada became apparent. She did not speak of her suffering, but she would sometimes get up in the night and light a holy candle in a transparent red glass cup. She would crouch beside it mumbling Spanish prayers with a hand pressed to her side where some pain was located. It made her furious when he got up or questioned her about it. She behaved as if she were suffering from some disgraceful secret. Mind your own business, she would snarl back at him if he asked, What is it? Hours later she would waken him again, crawling back into bed with an exhausted sigh which told him that the attack of pain had subsided. Then, moved by pity, he would turn to her slowly and press her to him as gently as possible so that his pressure wouldn't renew the pain. She would not go to a doctor. She said she had been to a doctor a long time ago and that he had told her she had a disease of the kidneys the same as her father had had and that there was nothing to do but try to forget it. It doesn't matter, she said, I am going to forget it.

She made an elaborate effort to conceal the attacks as they became more frequent and more severe, thinking perhaps that her illness would disgust him and he might forsake her completely. She would steal out of bed so cautiously that it would take her five or ten minutes to disengage herself from the covers and creep to the chair in the corner, and if she lit the prayer candle, she would crouch over it with cupped hands to conceal the flame. It was evident to Kamrowski that the infection in her body, whatever it was, was now passing from a chronic into an acute stage. He would have been more concerned if he had not just then started to work on another novel. The girl Amada began to exist for him on the other side of a center which was his writing. Everything outside of that existed in a penumbra as shadowy forms on the further side of a flame. Days and events were uncertain. The ringing of the doorbell and the telephone was ignored. Eating became irregular. He slept with his clothes on, sometimes in the chair where he worked. His hair grew long as a hermit's. He grew a beard and mustache. A lunatic brightness appeared in his eyes while his ordinarily smooth face acquired hollows and promontories and his hands shook. He had fits of coughing and palpitations of the heart which sometimes made him think he was dying and greatly speeded up his already furious tempo of composition.

Afterwards he could not remember clearly how things had been between himself and Amada during this feverish time. He ceased to make love to her, he ceased that altogether, and he was only dimly aware of her presence in the apartment. He gave her commands as if she were a servant and she obeyed them quickly and wordlessly with an air of fright. Get me coffee! he would suddenly yell at her. Play that record again, he would say, with a jerk of his thumb at the Victrola. But he was not conscious of her except as a creature to carry out such commissions.

During this interval she had quit stealing his money. Most of the day she would sit at the opposite end of the wide front room in which he was working. As long as she stayed at that end of the room, her presence did not distract him from his work, but if she entered unbidden his half of the room or if she asked him some question, he would yell at her furiously or even hurl a book at her. She became very quiet. When she went to the kitchen or bathroom, she would move one foot at a time, slowly and stealthily, gazing back at him to make sure he had no objection. Her face had changed, too, in the same way that his had changed. The long equine face had become even bonier than before and dreadfully sallow and the eyes now glittered as if they looked into a room where a great light was. She moved about with an odd stateliness which must have come from the suffering caused by the movement. One hand was now always pressed to the side that hurt her and she moved with exaggerated uprightness in defiance of the temptation to ease her discomfort by crouching. These details of her appearance he could not have noticed at the time, not consciously, and yet they came to him vividly in recollection. It was only afterwards, too, that he troubled himself to wonder how she might have interpreted this disastrous change in their way of living together. She must have thought that all affectionate feeling for her was gone and that he was now enduring her company out of pity only. She stopped stealing his money at night. For a month she sat in the corner and watched him, watched him with the dumb, wanting look of an animal in pain. Occasionally she would dare to cross the room. When he seemed to be resting from his labor, she would come to his side and run her fingers inquiringly down his body to see if he desired her, and finding out that he didn't, she would retire again speechlessly to her side of the room.

Then all at once she left him. He had spent a night out with his new blond mistress and returned to find that Amada had packed her locker-trunk and removed it from the apartment, this time in grim earnest. He made no attempt to find her. He believed that she would necessarily return of her own accord, for he could not imagine her being able to do otherwise. But she did not return to him, as the days passed, nor did any word of her reach him. He was not certain how he felt about this. He thought for a while that he might even be somewhat relieved by the resulting simplification of his life and the absence of that faint odor of disease which had lately hung sadly over the bed they had slept in. There was still always the book, sometimes loosening its grip now that the first draft was finished, but still making him insensible as a paranoiac to everyday life. During the intervals when the work dropped off, when there was discouragement or a stop for reflection, Kamrowski would take to the streets and follow strange women. He glutted his appetite with a succession of women and continually widened the latitude of his experience, till, all at once, he was filled with disgust at himself and the circus-trapeze of longing on which he had kicked himself senselessly back and forth since the flight of the girl he had lived with. He didn't want any more of that now or ever.

And so one night, about five months after their separation, the image of Amada stalked with a sound of trumpets through the midnight walls of his apartment. She stood like some apparition of flame at the foot of his bed, all luminous from within as an X-ray picture. He saw the tall white bones of her standing there, and he sat bolt upright in the sweat-dampened covers and gave a loud cry; then he fell back on his face to weep uncontrollably till the coming of morning. When daylight was coming, even before the windows had turned really white, he rose to pack his valise and arrange for the trip to Laredo, to find the lost girl and bring her back into the empty room in his heart. He assumed without thinking that Laredo was where she would be, because it was where he had found her.

He was not wrong about that. She had returned to Laredo five months ago but not to the Texas Star where he had found her. The manager of the hotel pretended to have no knowledge of the girl, but the Mexican porter told him that he would find her in the home of her family on the outskirts of town, in a house without number on a street without name, at the bottom of a steep hill on which stood an ice plant.

When Kamrowski arrived at the door of the gray wooden house to which these directions took him — a building no more than a shack which leaned exhaustedly on the edge of a steep and irregular road of gray dust — all of the female family came to the door and talked excitedly among themselves, brushing him avidly up and down with their eyes, half smiling and half snarling at him like a pack of wild dogs. They seemed to be arguing almost hysterically among themselves as to whether or not this stranger should be admitted. He was so sick with longing to see the lost girl that he could not bring out the little Spanish he knew. All he could say was Amada, more and more loudly. And then all at once, from some recess of the building, a loud, hoarse voice was lifted like the crow of a cock. It had a ring of anger but the word called out was the affectionate name she used to call him. Rubio, which meant blond. He swept past the women, brushing them aside with both arms, and made for the direction from which the fierce call had come. He fairly hurled himself against the warped door and broke into a room which was all dark except for a vigil light in a red glass cup. He looked that way where the light in the glass cup was. There he saw her. She was lying upon a pallet arranged upon the bare floor.

It was impossible to judge her appearance in the windowless room, a sort of storage closet, with that one candle burning, especially since he had just come in from the glare of a desert sunset. He made out, gradually, that she was wearing a man's undershirt and he noticed how big her hands and her elbows were now that the arms were so emaciated, and her head seemed almost as big as the head of a horse and the familiar, coarse hair was hanging like a horse's mane about her scrawny neck and shoulders. His first emotion was fury as well as pity. What does this mean, what are you doing in here? he cried out fiercely. Mind your own business, she yelled back at him, exactly as ;f they had never been separated. Then he swallowed his rage at her family, still going on with their high-pitched argument beyond the door he had slammed shut. He crouched on his haunches beside the pallet and took hold of her hand. She tugged away from his grasp but not quite strongly enough to break it. She seemed to be trying to seem more alive than she was. She did not let herself entirely back down on the pallet, although he could see it was an effort for her to remain propped up on her elbow. And she did not allow her voice to drop but kept it at the same loud and harsh pitch. She did not remove her eyes

140

from his face which she seemed to be straining to examine, but she did not return his look directly. She seemed to be staring at his nose or his mouth. There was a great bewilderment in her look, a wonder at his being there, at his coming to see her. She asked him several times, What are you doing here in Laredo? And his answer, I came here to see you, did not seem to satisfy her. At last he leaned over and touched her shoulder and said, You ought to lie back. She glared at him fiercely. I am all right, she said. Her dark eyes were now immense. All of the light that came from the ruby glass cup was absorbed in those eyes and magnified into a beam that shot into his heart and deprived that moonlike organ of all its shadows, exposing in brutal relief the barrenness of it the way that the moon's landscape, with the sun full on it, turns into a hard and flat disk whose light is borrowed. He could not endure it. He sprang from beside the pallet. He dug in his pocket and pulled out a handful of bills. Take these, he whispered hoarsely. He tried to stuff them into her hands. I don't want your money, she answered. Then after a slight pause she muttered, Give it to them. She jerked her head toward the door beyond which the family were now preparing noisily for supper. He felt defeated altogether. He sighed and looked down at his hands. Her own hands lifted, then, and reached falteringly toward his head. Rubio, she whispered, the word for blond. Tiredly one of her hands dropped down his body to see if he desired her, and discovering that he did not, she smiled at him sadly and let her eyes fall shut. She seemed to be falling asleep; so then he leaned over and kissed her gently at the edge of her large mouth. Morena, he whispered, which was the word for dark one. Instantly the long bony arms flung about him an embrace which took his breath. She pressed their faces painfully together, her Indian cheekbones bruising his softer flesh. Scalding tears and the pressure of those gaunt arms broke finally all the way through the encrusted shell of his ego, which had never before been broken all the way through, and he was released. He was let out of the small but apparently rather light and comfortable room of his known self into a space that lacked the comfort of limits. He entered a space of bewildering dark and immensity, and yet not dark, of which light is really the darker side of the sphere. He was not at home in it. It gave him unbearable fright, and so he crawled back.

He crawled back out of the gaunt embrace of the girl. I will come back in the morning, he said to the girl as he rose from beside the pallet and crawled back into the small room he was secure in . . .

When he returned in the morning, the atmosphere of his reception was different. There was an air of excitement in the place that he could not fathom, and all of the women seemed to have on their best clothes. He thought perhaps it was because of the money that he had left in the sickroom. He started to cross to that room, but the old woman plucked his sleeve and pointed toward another. She led him into the parlor of the house and he was astonished to find that they had moved the girl there. Because he did not understand their speech, he could not realize at first that she had died in the night; this he did not realize until he had picked up her hand, nearly as dark as a Negro's, and found it cool and stiffened. They had dressed her in white, a nightgown of clean white linen that shone with starch, and when he released the hand, the oldest woman advanced and placed it carefully back in its former position on the flat bosom.

He noticed also that the odor of sickness was gone, or possibly lost in the odor of burning wax, for a great many candles had been brought into the room and set in ruby glass cups on the window ledges. The blinds had been lowered against the meridian glare of the flat desert country, but the glare filtered through pin-point perforations in the old fabric so that each blind was like a square of green sky with stars shining in it. The mourners assembled there were mostly neighbors' children, the smallest ones naked, the larger dressed in gray rags. One little girl was holding a homemade doll, roughly cut out of wood and painted into a grotesque semblance of human infancy. Coarse black hair had been attached to the head. It seemed somehow like an effigy of the dead girl. Unable to look upon the actual face and its now intolerable mystery, Kamrowski stole to the side of the half-naked child and gently and timidly thrust his hand toward the doll. He touched the coarse black hair of the doll with a finger. The child complained faintly and hugged the doll closer to her. Kamrowski began to tremble. He felt that his hand must keep in touch with the doll. He must not let the child move away with her precious possession, and so with one hand he stroked the head of the child while with the other hand's finger he kept in touch with the familiar black hair. But still the child edged away, withdrawing from his caress and regarding him with huge distrustful brown eyes.

Meanwhile a whispered consultation seemed to be going on among the women. It grew louder with excitement and finally the grandmother, with an abrupt decision, separated herself from the group and approached Kamrowski and cried out to him in English, Where is Amada's money, where is her money?

He stared at the old woman stupidly. What money? She made a fierce spitting noise as she thrust toward him a handful of yellow papers. He looked down at them. They seemed to be telegraph forms. Yes, they were all money orders, sent from the city in which he had lived with Amada. The sums were those she had stolen at night from his pockets.

Kamrowski looked wildly about for a way to escape. The women were closing about him like a wolf pack, now all jabbering at once. He made for the outer door. Beside the door the little girl with the doll appeared to him dimly. Impulsively he reached out and snatched the doll from the child as he ran past her into the dusty brilliance of the road. He ran as fast as he could up the steep and irregular dirt road with the wailing child running behind him, feeling only a need of hanging onto the child's grotesque plaything till he was alone somewhere and able to cry.

THE MATTRESS BY THE
TOMATO PATCH

THE MATTRESS
by the TOMATO
PATCH

My landlady, Olga Kedrova, has given me a bowl of ripe tomatoes from the patch that she lies next to, sunning herself in the great white and blue afternoons of California. These tomatoes are big as my fist, bloody red of color, and firm to the touch as a young swimmer's pectoral muscles.

I said, Why, Olga, my God, it would take me a month to eat that many tomatoes, but she said, Don't be a fool, you'll eat them like grapes, and that was almost how I ate them. It is now five o'clock of this resurrected day in the summer of 1943, a day which I am recording in the present tense although it is ten years past. Now there are only a couple of the big ripe tomatoes left in the pale-blue china bowl, but their sweetness and pride are undimmed, for their heart is not in the bowl which is their graveyard but in the patch that Olga lies next to, and the patch seems to be inexhaustible. It remains out there in the sun and the loam and in the consanguine presence of big Olga Kedrova. She rests beside the patch all afternoon on a raggedy mattress retired from service in one of her hotel bedrooms.

This resurrected day is a Saturday and all afternoon pairs of young lovers have wandered the streets of Santa Monica, searching for rooms to make love in. Each uniformed boy holds a small zipper bag and the sun-pinked-or-gilded arm of a pretty girl, and they seem to be moving in pools of translucent water. The girl waits at the foot of steps which the boy bounds up, at first eagerly, then anxiously, then with desperation, for Santa Monica is literally flooded with licensed and unlicensed couples in this summer of 1943. The couples are endless and their search is unflagging. By sundown and long after, even as late as two or three in the morning, the boy will bound up steps and the girl wait below, some-times primly pretending not to hear the four-letter word he mutters after each disappointment, sometimes saying it for him when he resumes his dogged hold on her arm. Even as daybreak comes they'll still be searching and praying and cursing with bodies that ache from pent-up longing more than fatigue.

Terrible separations occur at daybreak. The docile girl finally loses faith or patience; she twists violently free of the hand that bruises her arm and dashes sobbing into an all-night café to phone for a cab. The boy hovers outside, gazing fiercely through fog and window, his now empty fist opening and closing on itself. She sits between two strangers, crouches over coffee, sobbing, sniffing, and maybe after a minute she goes back out to forgive him and rests in his arms without hope of anything private, or maybe she is relentless and waits for the cab to remove her from him forever, pretending not to see him outside the fogged window until he wanders away, drunk now, to look for more liquor, turning back now and then to glare at the hot yellow pane that shielded her from his fury. Son of a bitch of a four-letter word for a part of her woman's body is muttered again and again as he stumbles across the car tracks into Palisades Park, under royal palm trees as tall as five-story buildings and over the boom of white breakers and into mist. Long pencils of light still weave back and forth through the sky in search of enemy planes that never come over and nothing else seems to move. But you never can tell. Even at this white hour he might run into something that's better than nothing before the paddy-wagon picks him up or he falls onto one of those cots for service men only at some place like the Elks' Lodge.

Olga knows all this, but what can she do about it? Build more rooms single-handed? To look at Olga you'd almost believe that she could. She is the kind of woman whose weight should be computed not in pounds but in stones, for she has the look of a massive primitive sculpture. Her origin is the Middle East of Europe. She subscribes to the *Daily Worker*, copies of which she sometimes thrusts under my door with paragraphs boxed in red pencil, and she keeps hopefully handing me works by Engels and Veblen and Marx which I hold for a respectful interval and then hand back to her with the sort of vague comment that doesn't fool her a bit. She has now set me down as a hopelessly unregenerate prostitute of the capitalist class, but she calls me "Tennie" or "Villyums" with undiminished good humor and there is nothing at all that she doesn't tell me about herself and nothing about myself that she doesn't expect me to tell . . . When I first came to stay here, late in the spring, and it came out in our conversation that I was a writer at Metro's, she said, Ha ha, I know you studio people! She says things like this with an air of genial complicity which a lingering reserve in my nature at first inclined me to pretend not to understand. But as the summer wore on, my reserve dropped off, and at present I don't suppose we have one secret between us. Sometimes while we are talking, she will go in my bathroom and continue the conversation with the door wide open and her seated figure in full view, looking out at me with the cloudlessly candid eyes of a child who has not yet learned that some things are meant to be private.

This is a house full of beds and I strongly suspect that big Olga has lain in them all. These big old-fashioned brass or white iron beds are like the keyboard of a concert grand piano on which she is running up and down in a sort of continual arpeggio of lighthearted intrigues, and I can't much blame her when I look at her husband. It is sentimental to think that all sick people deserve our sympathy. Ernie is sick but I can't feel sorry for him. He is a thin, sour man whose chronic intestinal trouble was diagnosed eight years ago as cancer, but whose condition today is neither much worse nor better than when the diagnosis was made, a fact that confirms the landlady's contempt for all opinions that don't come through "The Party."

Ernie does the woman's work around the apartment-hotel, while Olga soaks up the sun on the high front steps or from the mattress by the tomato patch out back. From those front steps her lively but unastonished look can comprehend the whole fantasy of Santa Monica Beach, as far north as the "Gone with the Wind" mansion of former film star Molly Delancey and as far south as the equally idiotic but somewhat gayer design of the roller coasters at Venice, California.

Somehow it seems to me, because I like to think so, that this is the summer hotel, magically transplanted from the Crimean seacoast, where Chekhov's melancholy writer, Trigorin, first made the acquaintance of Madame Arcadina, and where they spent their first weekend together, sadly and wisely within the quiet sound of the sea, a pair of middle-aged lovers who turn the lights off before they undress together, who read plays aloud to each other on heaps of cool pillows and sometimes find that the pressure of a hand before falling asleep is all that they really need to be sure they are resting together.

The Palisades is a big white wooden structure with galleries and gables and plenty of space around it. It stands directly over a municipal playground known as "Muscle Beach." It is here that the acrobats and tumblers work out in the afternoons, great powerful Narcissans who handle their weightless girls and daintier male partners with a sort of tender unconsciousness under the blare and activity of our wartime heavens.

While I am working at home, during my six-week lay-off-without-pay from the studio (a punishment for intransigence that presages a short term of employment and forces me to push my play anxiously forward), it is a comfort now and then to notice Big Olga dreaming on the front steps or sprawled on that old mattress in back of the building.

I like to imagine how the mattress got out there . . . This is how I see it.

On one of those diamond-bright mornings of early summer, Big Olga looms into an upstairs bedroom a soldier and his girl-friend have occupied for the week-end which has just passed. With nonchalant grunts, she looks at the cigarette stains and sniffs at the glasses on the bed-side table. With only a token wrinkle or two of something too mild to be defined as disgust, she picks up the used contraceptives tossed under the bed, counts them and murmurs "My God" as she drops them into the toilet and comes back out of the bathroom without having bothered to wash her hands at the sink. The boy and the girl have plainly enjoyed themselves and Olga is not the kind to resent their pleasure and she is philosophical about little damages to beds and tables incurred in a storm of love-making. Some day one of them will fall asleep or pass out in bed with a lighted cigarette and her summer hotel will burn down. She knows this will happen some day but till it happens, oh, well, why worry about it.

She goes back to the bed and jerks off the crumpled sheets to expose the mattress.

My God, she cries out, the condition this mattress is in!

Bad? says Ernie.

Completely ruined, she tells him.

Pigs, says Ernie.

But Olga is not unhappy.

Pigs, pigs, pigs, says Ernie with almost squealing repugnance, but Olga says, Aw, shut up! A bed is meant to make love on, so why blow your stack about it?

This shuts Ernie up, but inwardly he boils and becomes short-winded.

Ernie, says Olga, you take that end of the mattress.

She picks up the other.

Where does it go? asks Ernie.

The little man backs toward the door but Olga thinks differently of it. She gives an emphatic tug toward the gallery entrance. This way, she says roughly, and Ernie, who rarely presumes anymore to ask her a question, tags along with his end of the mattress dragging the carpet. She kicks the screen door open and with a joyous gasp she steps out into the morning above the ocean and beach. The white clocktower of downtown Santa Monica is looking out of the mist, and everything glistens. She sniffs like a dog at the morning, grins connivingly at it, and shouts, Around this way!

The mattress is lugged to the inland side of the gallery, and Ernie is still not aware of what she is up to.

Now let go, says Olga.

Ernie releases his end and staggers back to the scalloped white frame wall. He is broken and breathless, he sees pinwheels in the sky. But Olga is chuckling a little.

153

While the pinwheels blinded him, Olga has somehow managed to gather both ends of the mattress into her arms and has rolled them together to make a great cylinder. Hmmm, she says to herself. She likes the feel of the mattress, exults in the weight of it on her. She stands there embracing the big inert thing in her arms and with the grip of her thighs. It leans against her, a big exhausted lover, a lover that she has pressed upon his back and straddled and belabored and richly survived. She leans back with the exhausted weight of the mattress resting on her, and she is chuckling and breathing deeply now that she feels her power no longer contested. Fifteen, twenty, twenty-five years are in her of life still, not depleted more than enough to make her calm and easy. Time is no problem to her. Hugging the mattress, she thinks of a wrestler named "Tiger" who comes and goes all summer, remembers a sailor named Ed who has spent some liberties with her, thinks of a Marine Sergeant, brought up in a Kansas orphanage, who calls her Mama, feels all the weight of them resting lightly on her as the weight of one bird with various hurrying wings, staying just long enough to satisfy her and not a moment longer. And so she grips the big mattress and loves the weight of it on her. Ah, she says to herself, ah, hmmm . . .

She sees royal palm trees and the white clocktower of downtown Santa Monica, and possibly says to herself, Well, I guess I'll have a hot barbecue and a cold beer for lunch at the Wop's stand on Muscle Beach and I'll see if Tiger is there, and if he isn't, I'll catch the five o'clock bus to L.A. and take in a good movie, and after that

I'll walk over to Olivera Street and have some tamales with chili and two or three bottles of Carta Blanca and come back out to the beach on the nine o'clock bus. That will be after sundown, and three miles east of the beach, they turn the lights out in the bus (because of the war-time blackout), and Olga will have chosen a good seat-companion near the back of the bus, a sailor who's done two hitches and knows the scoop, so when the lights go out, her knees will divide and his will follow suit and the traveling dusk will hum with the gossamer wings of Eros. She'll nudge him when the bus slows toward the corner of Wilshire and Ocean. They'll get off there and wander hand-in-hand into the booming shadows of Palisades Park, which Olga knows like a favorite book never tired of. All along that enormously tall cliff, under royal palms and over the Pacific, are little summer houses and trellised arbors with benches where sudden acquaintances burst into prodigal flower.

All of these things, these prospects, too vivid to need any thought, are in her nerves as she feels the weight of the mattress between her breasts and thighs, and now she is ready to show the extent of her power. She tightens the grip of her arms on the soft-hard bulk and raises the mattress to the height of her shoulders.

Watch out, my God, says Ernie, you'll rupture your-self!

Not I! says Olga, I'll not rupture myself!

Ha ha, look here! she orders.

Her black eyes flash as she coils up her muscles.

One for the money, two for the show, three to get ready, and four to GO!

Christ Almighty, says Ernie without much breath or conviction, as the mattress sails, yes, almost literally sails above the rail of the gallery and out into the glistening air of morning. Fountains of delicate cotton fiber spurt out of at least a thousand ruptures in its cover the moment the wornout mattress plops to the ground.

Hmmm, says Olga.

The act has been richly completed. She grips the rail of the gallery with her hands that have never yet been fastened on anything they could not overwhelm if they chose to. The big brass bangles she has attached to her ears are jingling with silly but rapturous applause, and Ernie is thinking again, as he has thought so often, since death so thoughtlessly planted a slow seed in his body: How is it possible that I ever lay with this woman, even so long ago as that now is!

With an animal's sense of what goes on behind it, Olga knows what her invalid husband feels when she exhibits her power, and her back to him is neither friendly nor hostile. And if tonight he has a cramp in the bowels that doubles him up, she'll help him to the bathroom and sit yawning on the edge of the tub with a cigarette and a Hollywood fan-magazine, while he sweats and groans on the stool. She'll utter goodhumored "phews" and wave her cigarette at the stench of his anguish, sometimes extending a hand to cup his forehead. And if he bleeds and collapses, as he sometimes does, she'll pick him up and carry him back to bed and fall asleep with his hot fingers twitching in hers, doing it all as if God had told her to do it. There are two reasons: He is a mean and sick little beast that once mated with her and would have been left and forgotten a long time ago except for the now implausible circumstance that she bore two offspring by him — a daughter employed as "executive secretary to a big wheel at Warner's." (She has to stay at his place because he's a lush and needs her constant attention.) And this one, "My God, look at him." A blownup Kodachrome snapshot of a glistening wet golden youth on some unidentified beach that borders a jungle. He makes his nakedness decent by holding a mass of red flowers before his groin. Olga lifts the picture and gives it five kisses as fast as machine-gun fire, which leave rouge-stains on the glass, as bright as the blossoms the grinning boy covers his sex with.

So those are the circumstances she feels behind her in Ernie, and yet they cast no shadow over the present moment. What she is doing is what is usual with her, she's thinking in terms of comfort and satisfaction as she looks down at the prostrate bulk of the mattress. Her eyes are soaking up the possibilities of it. The past of the mattress was good. Olga would be the last to deny its goodness. It has lain beneath many summers of fornications in Olga's summer hotel. But the future of the mattress is going to be good, too. It is going to lie under Olga on afternoons of leisure and under the wonderful rocking-horse weather of Southern California.

That is what the veteran mattress has done for the past few summers. The rain and the sun have had their influence on it. Unable to dissolve and absorb it into themselves, the elements have invested it with their own traits. It is now all softness and odors of ocean and earth, and it is still lying next to the prodigal patch of tomatoes that make me think of a deck of green-backed cards in which everything but diamonds and hearts have been thrown into discard.

(What do you bid? demands the queen of hearts. But that is Olga, and Olga is bidding *forever!*)

On afternoons of leisure she lies out there on this over-blown mattress of hers and her slow-breathing body is steamed and relaxed in a one-piece sarong-type garment that a Hollywood pinup girl would hardly dare to appear in. The cocker spaniel named Freckles is resting his chin on her belly. He looks like a butterscotch pudding with whipped cream on it. And these two indolent creatures drift in and out of attention to what takes place in Olga's summer hotel. The quarrels, the music, the wailing receipt of bad news, the joyful shouting, everything that goes on is known and accepted. Without even feeling anything so strong as contempt, their glances take in the activities of the husband having words with a tenant about a torn window shade or sand in a bathtub or wet tracks on the stairs. Nobody pays much attention to poor little Ernie. The Ernies of the world are treated that way. They butt their heads against the walls of their indignation until their dry little brains are shaken to bits. There he goes now, I can see him out this window, trotting along the upstairs gallery of the projecting back wing of the building with some linen to air, some bedclothes on which young bodies have taken their pleasure, for which he hates them. Ernie treats everyone with the polite fury of the impotent cuckold, and they treat Ernie in such an offhand manner it turns him around like a top till he runs down and stops. Sometimes while he complains, they walk right past him dripping the brine of the ocean along the stairs, which Ernie must get down on his hands and knees to wipe up. Pigs, pigs, is what he calls them, and of course he is right, but his fury is too indiscriminate to be useful. Olga is also capable of fury, but she reserves it for the true beast which she knows by sight, sound, and smell, and although she has no name for it, she knows it is the beast of mendacity in us, the beast that tells mean lies, and Olga is not to be confused and thrown off guard by smaller adversaries. Perhaps all adversaries are smaller than Olga, for she is almost as large as the afternoons she lies under.

And so it goes and no one resists the going.

The wonderful rocking-horse weather of California goes rocking over our heads and over the galleries of Olga's summer hotel. It goes rocking over the acrobats and their slim-bodied partners, over the young cadets at the school for flyers, over the ocean that catches the blaze of the moment, over the pier at Venice, over the roller coasters and over the vast beach-homes of the world's most successful kept women — not only over those persons and paraphernalia, but over all that is shared in the commonwealth of existence. It has rocked over me all summer, and over my afternoons at this green and white checkered table in the yellow gelatine flood of a burlesque show. It has gone rocking over accomplishments and defeats; it has covered it all and absorbed the wounds with the pleasures and made no discrimination. For nothing is quite so cavalier as this horse. The giant blue rocking-horse weather of Southern California is rocking and rocking with all the signs pointing forward. Its plumes are smoky blue ones the sky can't hold and so lets grandly go of . . .

And now I am through with another of these afternoons so I push the chair back from the table, littered with paper, and stretch my cramped spine till it crackles and rub my fingers gently over a dull pain in my chest, and think what a cheap little package this is that we have been given to live in, some rubbery kind of machine not meant to wear long, but somewhere in it is a mysterious tenant who knows and describes its being. Who is he and what is he up to? Shadow him, tap his wires, check his intimate associates, if he has any, for there is some occult purpose in his coming to stay here and all the time watching so anxiously out of the windows . . .

Now I am looking out of a window at Olga who has been sunning herself on that smoking-car joke of a mattress the whole livelong afternoon, while she ages at leisure and laps up life with the tongue of a female bull. The wrestler Tiger has taken the room next to mine, that's why she keeps looking this way, placidly alert for the gleam of a purple silk robe through his window curtains, letting her know of his return from the beach, and before he has hung the robe on a hook on the door, the door will open and close as softly as an eyelid and Olga will have disappeared from her mattress by the tomato patch. Once the cocker spaniel had the impudence to sniff and bark outside Tiger's door and he was let in and tossed right out the back window, and another time I heard Tiger muttering, Jesus, you fat old cow, but only a few moments later the noises that came through the wall made me think of the dying confessions of a walrus.

And so it goes and no one resists the going.

The perishability of the package she comes in has cast on Olga no shadow she can't laugh off. I look at her now, before the return of Tiger from Muscle Beach, and if no thought, no knowledge has yet taken form in the protean jelly-world of brain and nerves, if I am patient enough to wait a few moments longer, this land-lady by Picasso may spring up from her mattress and come running into this room with a milky-blue china bowl full of reasons and explanations for all that exists.

THE COMING OF SOMETHING
TO THE WIDOW HOLLY

THE COMING of SOMETHING to the WIDOW HOLLY

THE widow Isabel Holly was a rooming-house owner. How she had come to be one she hardly knew. It had crept up on her the same as everything else. She had an impression, however, that this was the house where she had lived as a bride. There had been, she also believed, a series of more or less tragic disappointments, the least of which had been Mr. Holly's decease. In spite of the fact that the late Mr. Holly, whose first name she could no longer remember, had left her with an adequate trust fund, she had somehow felt compelled at one time or another to open her house on Bourbon Street in New Orleans to persons regarding themselves as "paying guests." In times more recent the payments had dwindled away and now it seemed that the guests were

really dependents. They had also dwindled in number.
She had an idea that there had once been many, but now
there were only three, two middle-aged spinsters and a
bachelor in his eighties. They got along not well together. Whenever they met on the stairs or in the hall
or at the door of the bathroom, there was invariably
some kind of dispute. The bolt on the bathroom door
was continually broken, repaired, and broken again. It
was impossible to keep any glassware about the place.
Mrs. Holly had finally resorted to the use of nothing but
aluminum in the way of portable fixtures. And while
objects of this material withstood shocks better themselves, they also inflicted considerably more damage on
whatever they struck. Time and again one of the terrible
three tenants would appear in the morning with a blood-
stained bandage about the head, a bruised and swollen
mouth or a blackened eye. In view of the circumstances
it was reasonable to suppose that they would, at least
one of them, move out of the premises. Nothing, however, seemed further from their intention. They clung
as leeches to their damp-smelling rooms. All were col-
lectors of things, bottle caps or matchboxes or tin-foil
wrappings, and the length of their tenancy was eloquently witnessed by the vast store of such articles stacked
about the moldy walls of their bedrooms. It would be
hard to say which of the three was the least desirable
tenant, but the bachelor in his eighties was certainly the
one most embarrassing to a woman of gentle birth and
breeding as Isabel Holly unquestionably had been and
was.

This octogenarian recluse had run up a great many

debts. The last few years he had seemed to be holding an almost continual audience with his creditors. They stamped in and out of the house, in and out, not only during the day but sometimes at the most unlikely hours of the night. The widow Holly's establishment was located in that part of the old French Quarter given over mostly to honky-tonks and bars. The old man's creditors were heavy drinkers, most of them, and when the bars closed against them at night, the liquor having inflamed their tempers, they would stop off at Mrs. Holly's to renew their relentless siege of her tenant, and if he declined to answer the loud ringing and banging at the door, missiles of various kinds were thrown through the panes of the windows wherever the shutters were fallen off or unfastened. In New Orleans the weather is sometimes remarkably good. When this was the case, the creditors of the old man were less obnoxious, at times merely presenting their bills at the door and marching quietly away. But when it was bad outside, when the weather was nasty, the language the creditors used in making demands was indescribably awful. Poor Mrs. Holly had formed the habit of holding her hands to her ears on days when the sun wasn't out. There was one particular tradesman, a man named Cobb who represented some mortician's establishment, who had the habit of using the worst epithet in the English language at the top of his voice, over and over again with increasing frenzy. Only the middle-aged women, Florence and Susie, could cope with the tradesman Cobb. When they acted together, he could be driven away, but only at the sacrifice of broken banisters.

The widow Holly had only once made any allusion to these painful scenes between the tradesman Cobb and her bachelor tenant. On that occasion, after a particularly disagreeable session in the downstairs hall, she had timidly inquired of the old man if some kind of settlement couldn't be reached with his friend from the undertakers.

Not till I'm dead, he told her.

And then he went on to explain, while bandaging his head, that he had ordered a casket, the finest casket procurable, that it had been especially designed and built for him — now the unreasonable Mr. Cobb wished him to pay for it, even before his decease.

This son of an illegitimate child, said the roomer, suspects me of being immortal! I wish it were true, he sighed, but my doctor assures me that my life expectancy is barely another eighty-seven years!

Oh, said poor Mrs. Holly.

Mild as her nature was, she was nearly ready to ask him if he expected to stay in the rooming house all that time — but just at this moment, one of the two indistinguishable female tenants, Florence or Susie, opened the door of her bedroom and stuck her head out.

This awful disturbance has got to stop! she yelled.

To emphasize her demand, she tossed an aluminum washbasin in their direction. It glanced off the head of the man who had ordered his casket and struck Mrs. Holly a terrible blow in the bosom. The octogenarian's head was bandaged with flannel, several layers of it, and padded with damp cardboard, so the blow did not hurt him nor even catch him off guard. But as Isabel

168

Holly fled in pain down the stairs to the cellar — her usual sanctuary — she glanced behind her to see the powerful old gentleman yanking a wooden post from the balustrade and shouting at Florence or Susie the very same unrepeatable word that the undertaker had used.

FOR PROBLEMS CONFER WITH
A. ROSE, METAPHYSICIAN!

This was the legend which Isabel Holly found on a business card stuck under her door facing Bourbon.

She went at once to the address of the consultant and found him seemingly waiting to receive her.

My dear Mrs. Holly, he said, you seem to be troubled.

Troubled? she said, Oh, yes, I'm terribly troubled. There seems to be something important left out of the picture.

What picture? he asked her gently.

My life, she told him.

And what is the element which appears to be missing?

An explanation.

Oh — an explanation! Not many people ask for *that* anymore.

Why? Why don't they? she asked.

Well, you see — Ah, but it's useless to tell you!

Then why did you wish me to come here?

The old man took off his glasses and closed a ledger.

My dear Mrs. Holly, he said, the fact of the matter is that you have a very unusual destiny in store. You are the first of your kind and character ever to be transplanted to this earth from a certain star in another universe!

169

And what is that going to result in?

Be patient, my dear. Endure your present trials as well as you can. A change is coming, a very momentous change, not only for you but for practically all others confined to this lunatic sphere!

Mrs. Holly went home and, before long, this interview, like everything else in the past, had faded almost completely out of her mind. The days behind her were like an unclear, fuzzy negative of a film that faded when exposed to the present. They were like a dull piece of thread she would like to cut and be done with. Yes, to be done with forever, like a thread from a raveled hem that catches on things when you walk. But where had she put the scissors? Where had she put away everything sharp in her life, everything which was capable of incision? Sometimes she searched about her for something that had an edge that she could cut with. But everything about her was rounded or soft.

The trouble in the house went on and on.

Florence Domingo and Susie Patten had quarreled. Jealousy was the reason.

Florence Domingo had an aged female relative who came to pay her a call about once a month, bringing an empty paper bag in the usually vain hope that Florence would give her something of relative value to take away in it. This indigent old cousin was extremely deaf, as deaf, you might say, as a fence pole, and consequently her conversations with Florence Domingo had to be carried on at the top of both their lungs, and since these conversations were almost entirely concerned with the other roomers at Mrs. Holly's, whatever degree of peace had prevailed under the roof before one of these visits was very drastically reduced right after one took place and sometimes even during its progress. Now Susie Patten never received a visitor and this comparative unpopularity of Susie's was not allowed to pass without comment by Florence and her caller.

How is old Susie Patten? the cousin would shriek.

Terrible. Same as ever, Florence would shout back.

Does she ever go out anywhere to pay a call? the cousin would yell.

Never, never! Florence would reply at the top of her lungs, and nobody comes to see her! She is a friendless soul, completely alone in the world.

Nobody comes to her?

Nobody!

Never?

Never! Absolutely *never!*

When the cousin got up to go, Florence Domingo would say to her, Now close your eyes and hold out your paper bag and see what you find in it when you get downstairs. This was her playful fashion of making a gift, and the old cousin was forbidden to look in the bag till she had left the house, and so great was her curiosity and her greed that she'd nearly break her neck in her rush to get out after the gift was presented. Usually it turned out to be a remnant of food of some kind, such as a half-eaten apple with the bitten places turned brown and withered about the edges where Florence had left her tooth marks, but once when the conversation had not gone to suit Miss Domino, it was the corpse of a rat that she had dropped in the held-out paper bag and the visits had been suspended for three months. But now the visits were going on again and the vexation of Susie Patten was well-nigh indescribable. Then an idea came to her. She launched a counteroffensive and a very clever one, too. Susie invented a caller of her own. Susie was very good at speaking in two voices: that is, she would speak in her own voice and then she would answer in a different one as if she were carrying on a conversation with someone. This invented caller of Susie's, moreover, was not an old woman. It was a gentleman who addressed her as Madam.

Madam, the invented caller would say, You are wearing your beautiful dotted Swiss today!

Oh, do you like it? Susie would cry out.

Yes, it goes with your eyes, the caller would tell her.

Then Susie would make kissing sounds with her mouth, first soft ones, then very loud ones, and then she would rock back and forth rapidly in her rocking-chair and go, Huff, huff, huff! And after a suitable interval she would cry out to herself, *Oh, no!* Then she would rock some more and go, Huff, huff, again, and presently, after another suitable pause, the conversation would be resumed and in due course it would turn to the subject of Florence Domingo. Disparaging comments would be made on the subject and also upon the subject of the Domingo collection of tin-foil wrappings and the Domingo's female relative with the paper bag held out for a gift when she left.

Madam, cried Susie's caller, that woman is not fit to live in a respectable house!

No, indeed, she is not, Susie would agree with him

loudly, and all this while Florence Domingo would be listening to every word that was spoken and every sound produced in the course of the long social call. Florence was only half sure that the caller existed, but she could not be completely sure that he didn't, and her doubt and uncertainty on this subject was extremely nerve-racking, and something really had to be done about it.

Something was done about it.

Isabel Holly, the widow who owned the building and suffered this — what shall we call it? — knew there was going to be trouble in the house when she saw Miss Domingo come in the front door one evening with a medium-sized box labeled EXPLOSIVES.

The widow Holly did not wait for eventualities that night. She went right out on the street, dressed as she was, in a pair of rayon bloomers and a brassière. She had hardly gotten around the corner when the whole block shook with a terrible detonation. She kept on running, shuddering in the cold, till she came to the park, the one beside the Cabildo, and there she knelt and prayed for several hours before she dared to turn back toward her home.

When Isabel Holly crept back to the house on Bourbon, she found it a shambles. The rooms were silent. But as she tiptoed past them, she saw here and there the bloody, inert, and hoarsely panting figures of easily twenty tradesmen including the ruffian Cobb. All over the floors and the treads of the stairs were little glittering objects which first she mistook for fragments of glass, but when she picked one up she found it to be a coin. Apparently money had been forthcoming from some quarter of the establishment, it had been cast around everywhere, but the creditors of the old man were still in no condition to gather it up. There must have been a great deal of violence preceding the money's disbursal.

Isabel Holly tried to think about this, but her brain was like a cracked vessel that won't hold water, and she was staggering with weariness. So she gave it up and dragged herself to her bedroom. In an envelope half thrust under the door she found a message which only increased the widow's mystification.

The message went as follows:

"My dear Mrs. Holly, I think that with my persuasion the ghastly disturbance has stopped. I am sorry I cannot wait till you return home as I am sure that you must feel a good deal of sorrow and confusion over conditions here. However I shall see you personally soon, and stay a good deal longer. Sincerely, Christopher D. Cosmos."

The weeks that followed were remarkably tranquil. All three of the incorrigible tenants remained locked in their rooms apparently in a state of intimidation. The violently paid-off creditors called at the house no more. The carpenters came and patched things up in silence. Telegraph messengers tiptoed up the stairs and rapped discreetly at the roomers' doors. Boxes began to be carried in and out — It soon appeared to Mrs. Holly's hardly believing mind that general preparations were being made by the terrible two and one to move from the premises.

As a matter of fact a bulletin corroborating this hopeful suspicion appeared in the downstairs hall not very long afterwards.

"We have decided," said this bulletin, "in view of your cousin's behavior, not to maintain our residence here any longer. This decision is absolutely inalterable and we would prefer not to discuss it. Signed: Florence Domingo, Susie Patten, Regis de Winter." (The signatures of the roomers.)

After her roomers' departure, Isabel Holly found it harder than ever to concentrate on things. Often during the day she would sit down worriedly at the kitchen table or on her unmade bed and clasp her forehead and murmur to herself, I've got to think, I've simply *got* to think! But it did no good, it did no good at all. Oh, yes, for a while she would *seem* to be thinking of something. But in the end it was always pretty much like a lump of sugar making strenuous efforts to preserve its integrity in a steamingly warm cup of tea. The cubic shape of a thought would not keep. It relaxed and dissolved and spread out flat on the bottom or drifted away.

At last one day she paid another visit to the house of the metaphysician. On his door was nailed a notice: "I've gone to Florida to stay young forever. Dear Love to all my enemies. Goodbye." She stared at it hopelessly for a moment and started to turn away. But just in the nick of time, a small white rodent squeezed from beneath the door and dropped at her feet an envelope sealed as the one that Christopher Cosmos had left at her house the time of the last disturbance. She tore it open and read the following message: "I have returned and am sleeping in your bedroom. Do not wake me up till after seven o'clock. We've had a long hard trip around the cape of the sun and need much rest before we start back again. Sincerely, Christopher D. Cosmos."

When Isabel Holly returned, there was, indeed, a sleeping man in her bedroom. She stood in the door and nearly stopped breathing with wonder. Oh, how handsome he was! He had on the uniform of a naval commander. The cloth was crisp and lustrous as deeply banked winter snow. The shoulders of the coat were braided; the braids were clasped to the garment with ruby studs. The buttons were aquamarine. And the chest of the man, exposed by the unbuttoned jacket, was burnished as fine, pale gold with diamond-like beads of perspiration on it.

He opened one eye and winked and murmured 'hello' and lazily rolled on his stomach and went back to sleep.

She couldn't decide what action she ought to take. She wandered vaguely about the house for a while, observing the changes which had occurred in her absence.

Everything now was put straight. It was all spick and span as if a regiment of servants had worked industriously for days, scrubbing and polishing, exacting a radiance from the dullest objects. Kitchen utensils worn away with rust and various other truck which could not be renovated had been thrown into or heaped beside an incinerator. GET RID OF THIS NONSENSE was scrawled on a laundry cardboard in the Commander's handwriting. Also among the stuff which her marvelous visitor had ordained for destruction were various relics of the late Mr. Holly, his stomach pump, the formidable bearded photograph of his mother in her daredevil outfit, the bucket of mutton tallow he greased himself with thrice weekly in lieu of bathing, the 970-page musical composition called *Punitive Measures* which he had striven tirelessly to master upon a brass instrument of his own invention — all of this reliquary truck was now heaped inside or beside the giant incinerator.

Wonders will never cease! the widow murmured as she returned upstairs.

A state of irresolution was not unfamiliar to the widow Holly, but this was the first time that it had made her light-footed as well as lightheaded. She rose to the chambers above with no effort of climbing, as a vapor rises from water into first morning light. There was not much light, not even in the parlor that fronted Bourbon Street, there was hardly more light than might have emanated from the uncovered chest of the slumbering young Commander in her bedroom. There was just light enough to show the face of the clock if she leaned toward it as if to invite a kiss. It was seven o'clock — so soon!

The widow did not have a cold, but as she folded some garments over a nest of pine cones in the parlor fireplace, she began to sniff. She sniffed again and again; all of the muscles under the surface of her chilly young skin began to quiver, for somewhere in the house, tremulous with moments coming and going as almost bodiless creatures might rush through a room made of nothing but doors, someone was surely holding a sugar-coated apple on a forked metal stick above a flame's rapid tongue, until the skin of it hissed and crackled and finally split open, spilling out sweet juices, spitting them into the flame and filling the whole house, now, all of the chill and dim chambers, upstairs and down, with an odor of celebration in the season of Advent.

THE VINE

THE
VINE

THE woman's body beside him while he slept was something he felt with the faint and thoughtless sentience of plants to sunlight: when it was gone, when she had left the bed, he knew the same blind, formless want that plants must feel without that warmth about them. While they slept there was a continuity between their bodies that he had grown to depend upon. In winter he never had quite heat enough in his own flesh; he always had to borrow a little from hers — there was always some contact between them, his knees curved into hers, his arm wrapped vinelike across her shoulders. But even when the nights were excessively warm, as they now were in late summer, his hand or his foot must remain in touch with some part of the woman. This was essential to his feeling of security. When the contact was broken, though he didn't awake, the comfort of sleep was lost and he turned fretfully this way and that, sometimes muttering her name aloud — *Rachel — Rachel*. If she was still in the room, she would return to the bed and then, her temporary loss having stirred in him a sleepy desire, he would take her body almost as a child takes the breast of its mother, a sort of blind, instinctive, fumbling possession that hardly emerged from the state of sleep — the way that plants expand into sunlight with that sweet, thoughtless gratitude that living matter feels for what sustains its being.

And so for some time now, with Rachel gone, he had slept unquietly. The cumulative, unsatisfied want drew him gradually out of sleep. His eyelids opened. Above him stretched a ceiling with a network of fine silver threads and memorized patches of brown from pipes that leaked in the rented rooms above. The square window admitted a harsh brilliance which was like the insolent stare of someone he knew despised him but which he could not escape from.

He closed his eyelids: pouted.

"Jesus, I feel like I've got a mouthful of old chicken feathers!"

Rachel said nothing.

He turned and saw that her side of the bed was empty. The covers were neatly folded back, the pillow smoothed out as though she hadn't slept there at all that night. For a moment he wondered stupidly if she had. Of course. His body that had recorded like an exposed film while his mind was sleeping gave back to him now the long, sweet history of her presence near him. And then he remembered also her restless tossing which kept him awake until he complained, "Rachel, why don't you lie still?" and she had said, "Oh, my God!" and he had said, "What?" and she had said nothing more — and he had then fallen asleep.

"Rachel."

The emptiness of the room replied to him with the desultory drone of a large horsefly; its wings flashed blue against the shining copper screen, as though his wife had been transformed into an insect.

Slightly grinning at this fantastic notion, he pushed himself up on his elbows and squinted about.

The prankish spirit of earlier years recurred sometimes in little tricks they played on each other, which made him think now that she might be hiding to tease him. But there was really not a place in the one-room apartment where a woman, even as tiny as Rachel, might conceal herself. The closet door was open; the kitchen alcove made a full confession from this angle.

Grunting, he bent over — saw beneath their folding bed the pale-blue garters he had lost but not his wife.

Through a series of hesitant, half-hearted movements, he got himself out of bed and over to their single window. Beyond its proscenium arch the world was presenting another hot day's beginning. The street, which was a street in the Village, was narrow and vacant: you might almost suppose that during the night a plague had wiped out the entire population. No, there was a figure, a woman, yes, but not Rachel, coming out of an areaway. He watched her pad mincingly to the delicatessen whose windows bore a chaos of whitewashed signs and price quotations. That was very likely where Rachel had gone, an empty milk bottle in a paper bag — how much had she taken of their small cash under the Dresden doll on the bureau? He went immediately to see, recalling the precise amount there had been when they went to bed. A quarter was missing. A phone call? And a subway fare? . . .

He chuckled a little uneasily: and then there was no longer anything to postpone the dreaded approach to the mirror. In his crumpled purple pajamas with white frogs on them, he moved anxiously to that soap-splashed glass over the sink to make the morning analysis of his looks. In his youth he had been very handsome indeed, an ideal juvenile type, and even at forty-three, not having permitted himself to exceed a ten-pound concession to middle years, he still had a fairly comfortable sense of being attractive. Ah, but his hair, they said it stopped thinning at forty and if you got it that far you had it for keeps. How true was this notion? He inclined his head as low as he could and still see into the glass. The crown was becoming more visible every day, yes, blooming forth pink as a rose. Ah, well. It was also said that thinning hair was a sign of superior male vigor. That could be; it cost him nothing to think so.

Automatically he began to rotate his scalp beneath the close grip of ten fingers, halting at the count of sixty with a breathless grunt of relief.

That completed, he went back to the window. He reached it just in time to see the spinsterish woman who had gone into the delicatessen coming back out of it bearing her package clasped tight against her flat bosom as though afraid that someone would snatch it from her. Have you ever noticed, he inquired of himself, how tightly anxious people hold onto things such as hatbrims while waiting in managers' offices? Huh! Yesterday when he walked out of McClintic's, his panama was so dented it had to be reblocked! Oh, yes. Now he knew what he had to do this morning. Call Edie Van Cleve about that part in the road company of *Violets Are Blue!* He took a dime and descended in his bathrobe to the downstairs hall. "Your reading was fine," she told him, "but Mr. Davidson feels you're a shade too young for the part." Going back up the stairs his heart jolted strangely. A palpitation. He had them off and on. The doctor had told him there was nothing organically wrong, no pathological lesion. "If you took your heart out," said the doctor, "you would find that it looked exactly like a normal heart, only a little overdeveloped because of the strenuous life that you've been leading." This statement was meant to be reassuring, more so than Donald had found it. What strenuous life? He had never overextended himself at work or at play. Rehearsals could be a strain. But he always felt fine while working. It was only during the last two or three years, that held these long periods of unwanted inaction, that he had begun to decline from the pink of condition.

Steps in the hall — *Rachel?* No, they continued upstairs . . .

He began to curse her, teasingly, as though she could hear him, his eyes fixed on the framed photograph of the Glow Worm Ballet, girls in shimmering tutus going

185

through some intricate dance routine. They had held tiny flashlights that winked off and on in the stage's rosy dusk. At the end of the line was Rachel, a shade smaller, quicker, and more graceful than the others. His act had followed hers. He was the straight man in a vulgar dialogue with a comedian now dead of heart disease. Tommy Watson. Huh. There was Tommy's picture. Kind of nice not having to compare it with the way he looked now. And there was his own picture in a straw hat and a bow tie. Not much older than his son would now be. But they had not had any children, he and Rachel. They had scrupulously avoided the chance of any for about ten years. And then one summer, about three years ago, Rachel had grown pensive. He couldn't snap her out of it. They were playing in summer stock. All at once Rachel had started looking her age, and the manager said, "I'm sorry but we can't light her anymore for ingénue parts, and we've got all the character women that we can use." That was a *horrible* thing. Rachel went around looking half conscious for a number of days. And then one night she said, "I want a baby." He demurred a little, but she was persistent. "We've got to have a baby." They stopped the preventive devices, and waited six months. And when it still didn't happen, they went to a doctor. Both were thoroughly examined, and at the end, the doctor talked to Rachel. Donald waited nervously outside. When she came out she looked at him sort of oddly.

"What did he say?"

"He says we can't have children."

"There's something wrong with you, honey?"

"Not with me," she told him. "He says *you're
sterile* . . ."

This had struck Donald a nasty blow where it hurts
a man most. The many flattering attentions which he
had received in his youth had inflated his sexual vanity
and it had never retracted to normal size.

On the way home from the doctor's he had been
flushed and silent. At last he said huskily:

"Rachel?"

"Yes?"

"Don't let anyone know."

"Don't be silly, Donald. It's nothing to be ashamed
of. But why advertise it?"

"Exactly . . ."

BUT their relations had been altered by the discovery.
They laughed to think what trouble they had taken all
those years to avoid something that couldn't have happened. But the joke was on Donald, really, and it was
hard to accept for that reason. For a while the psychic
trauma was so acute that he found it difficult to make
love to Rachel. But Rachel understood it better than he.
She won him tenderly back and gradually the humilia-
tion faded from his mind and things became almost the
same as they had been before. Donald was not inclined
to keep old hurts alive, and if Rachel was still brooding
about her disappointment, she wore no outward sign of
it. Donald got a fairly good part in a show that ran nine
months in New York, and they saved a bit of money.
When it went on the road, it perished under Claudia
Cassidy's incorruptible justice in Chicago. Since that

engagement Donald had had nothing but TV and not much of that.

Donald had once read somewhere that the way to combat a feeling of depression was to take unusual pains with your appearance. "Dress Your Blues Away" was the stimulating title of this column of advice; he remembered having read it aloud to Rachel during a time when she seemed to be giving in to her moods. It had been addressed to female readers, but there was nothing about the theory that was not adaptable to a youngish middle-aged man who took a better than normal pride in presenting a good appearance, and so he took out Rachel's manicure set and cleaned and trimmed and polished his nails; he powdered his plumpish body with lilac talcum and applied cologne to his armpits, donned a fresh pair of faintly pink-tinted nylon boxer's shorts, and removed from its laundryman's sheath one of a pair of snow-white linen suits that he had been husbanding all summer against some days of importance that hadn't arrived. "I've never known a man that looks as good as you in white linen," someone had said to him once. But that was in another country and the wench was dead, for when he actually caught a full-length view of himself, outside, on the dazzlingly unreal streets, in one of those sudden mirrors sandwiched between shop-windows, he saw that the tightness which he felt in the linen and which he thought might be attributable only to its laundered crispness was indisputably owing to the expansion about his middle. He tried unbuttoning the jacket: this felt better, but when he passed another sidewalk mirror, he noticed that the starched jacket now flared behind him in a way that made him look like a bantam rooster strutting along the street in snowy feathers. It took no more than this to undo all he had done to "dress away his blues," and as he continued aimlessly through noonday brilliance, through crowds that all seemed to have appointments to keep, definite places to go, he noticed that no one seemed to be looking at him and this was something that he had never noticed before and he tried deliberately to catch the eyes of people moving in the opposite stream on the walk. He slowed his walk and stared hard into faces looming toward him, not only the faces of pretty girls tripping out for lunch hour, but faces of women of his own generation, and with mounting dismay, a feeling close to a beginning of panic, he failed to hold their attention for more than a second and one girl, as she passed him, uttered a startled laugh, not necessarily at him, but if not at him, at what? She was walking alone . . .

He turned, directly after this experience, into a drugstore and ordered a bicarbonate of soda which he seized the instant the boy at the counter released it and drained it down without pause. Ah, that did relieve the gaseous compression which he felt under his heart, and that irritable organ seemed to beat more evenly than it had on the street. The city is full, he said to himself, of people that talk and laugh to themselves on the street, it is full of completely self-centered people capable only of seeing themselves in mirrors, and even if strangers don't gaze at you on the sidewalk as they once did, a summer or two gone by, that means only — that means only — *what?* — he failed to complete the reflection, having observed that the stool next to his at the soda fountain was now occupied by a girl whom he judged to be a young stenographer having her midday coke; she was probably dieting to keep her hips down, yes, they lapped somewhat over the chromium periphery of the stool, somewhat overhanging it like the hood of a mushroom, yes, he murmured encouragingly to himself as he met her eyes in the mirror at the moment when his fingers, the knuckles of his right hand, came gently into contact with her left buttock and gave it a couple of slight nudges. Her eyes blinked in the mirror but she continued to sip her coke without smiling or turning toward him. The blink and the unchanged expression were an equivocal reaction and so he tried it once more.

The woman did not turn toward him, there was still no change in her expression, but she began to speak to him in a low, rapid voice like the buzz of a swarm of stinging insects.

He preferred not to hear what she was saying to him, and he got up with a rapidity that made his head swim and charged out the door.

He consoled himself, or tried to console himself, with the observation that the Village now was overrun with women who hated men.

He knew not where he was going, but he was headed toward Washington Square.

Whew!!

He stopped.

He was in front of the Whitney Museum . . .

Boom, boom, boom, boom, boom, went that abused organ, his heart! Abused by what? "Tensions of his profession," said the doctor . . .

Boom, boom, boom . . .

In front of the museum was a cheerfully colored poster advertising a showing of nonobjective paintings . . .

Rachel . . .

What she had probably left somewhere in their room was a little note explaining that she had gone to spend the day with one of her girl friends, perhaps with Jane Austin, the one that lived uptown, on Columbus Circle, one that was equally friendly to them both. Well —

A pair of youngsters, a boy and a girl of the long-haired Village crowd, came up alongside him and also stared at the poster, and he moved over a little, respectfully, to hear their comments. He recognized the name Mondrian as one he had heard before, but the reproduction was still meaningless to him as a strip of linoleum in a clean, bright kitchen. There was a whole world of such things to which he had no entrance, and though he was vain, he was humble at heart, and never socced at enthusiasms to which he was an outsider. He stood there respectfully listening to the young couple's comments and then, God help him, the bicarb erupted in a belch so loud that the kids turned and burst into giggles!

He wasn't yet recovered from his lightheaded spell but had to move on . . .

Arrived at the Square, he caught a Fifth Avenue bus to Jane Austin's apartment, but there was no upper deck and it seemed to him, with disturbing vagueness, that maybe it had been a long time since there had been open-deck buses on Fifth Avenue; he couldn't remember if they still had them or not, and —

Thoughts trailed off without distinct ends or beginnings.

JANE was at home with a white cloth tied about her somewhat large-featured head, which look startled at him when she opened the door. Her greeting was an odd one; she said, "Get you!" and though he supposed it was an allusion to the white linen suit and mermaid-figured pale-blue and white silk tie, it wasn't as pleasant and warm a greeting as a caller might hope for.

"Rachel here?" he demanded heartily.

"Why, no! Should she be here?"

"Well, I thought maybe —"

"I haven't seen you or Rachel since that party in June."

He thought there was something a little too clipped and short-winded in her speech, and she didn't even apologize for her appearance. Evidently she had not suffered from depression that morning, or if she had, she had certainly no faith in the "Dress Your Blues Away" theory, but to give the devil her due, she was at least making some efforts to clean up the mess and disorder remaining from what must have been a very large party last night, to which, for some reason, she had omitted to ask them. But then New York is a place where everybody knows too many people . . .

He waited a moment for Jane to say, Sit down, and since she didn't, he walked casually past her and settled himself on the sofa.

He thought about the party last month, wondering if it contained some clue to Jane's altered attitude toward him. There had been a good deal of indiscriminate lechery, the sort of thing that Rachel never took part in but which he sometimes did, no more seriously than a man might join a bunch of kids playing baseball. Rachel had left early with a married couple, but he had stayed on. He remembered now that he and Jane and some other person had drifted into the bedroom and there had been some rather involved goings-on, in the course of which someone had gotten sore at someone and made a scene, he didn't remember about what or how it turned out except that he left soon after and stayed in a bar till it closed. Maybe the fight had been more serious than he recalled its having been. That would explain why Jane was behaving so coldly.

"Rachel has disappeared," he said to Jane.

"When?"

"This morning."

"Did she?"

Her manner expressed no interest. The room was filled with the musty flavor of dust and heat and liquor and stale tobacco. He waited for Jane to offer him a drink. He saw at least one bottle of Haig & Haig which had several fingers of liquor still left in it. But Jane was being obtuse. She leaned on the handle of the vacuum with a slight frown and a faraway look. She lived by herself in this unpleasantly bright apartment. Donald could never quite imagine people living alone. It seemed less conceivable, somehow, than life on the moon. How did they get up in the morning? How did they know when to eat, or where or how did they make up their minds about any of the little problems of existence? When you came home alone after being alone on the street, how was it bearable not having someone to tell all the little things you had on your mind? When you really thought about it, when you got down to it, what was there to live for outside the all-encompassing and protecting intimacy of marriage? And yet a great many women like Jane Austin got on without it. There were also men who got on without it. But he, he could not think of it! Going to bed alone, the wall on one side of you, empty space on the other, no warmth but your own, no flesh in contact with yours! Such loneliness was indecent! No wonder people who lived those obscenely solitary lives did things while sober that *you* only did when drunk . . .

He looked at Jane and felt kind of sorry for her, although she was certainly not being very nice to him today.

Well, she probably felt a little neglected. He should have called her or made some further advances after those blurred goings-on in the bedroom that night.

His ears were abruptly assailed by the renewed whine of the vacuum cleaner.

"Jane!"

"Excuse me just a few minutes. I'm expecting company and I've got things to redd up a little."

She gave him a quick, hard smile as she pushed the infernal apparatus across the floor. The odor became more and more nauseating. He raised his legs from the floor and stretched full-length on the sofa.

This sort of treatment he certainly would not put up with!

"Jane — *Jane!*"

She turned off the cleaner.

"What *is* it?"

"I'm feeling lonesome," he said.

"Are you?"

"Jane, don't you ever feel lonesome?"

"Never."

"Why don't you settle down, Jane?"

"What do you mean?"

"Get married!"

"*Hanh!*"

She started to turn on the vacuum. He grabbed it from her and rested his chin on the handle.

She put her hands on her hips and stared at him so uncordially that he was almost intimidated.

"Where do you think Rachel is?"

"Worried about her?"

"Oh, no," he laughed, "I'm not optimistic enough to think she's gone for good!"

Jane did not smile nor even glance at him again. She pushed the cleaner into a closet and began pounding the silk pillows into shape. She tugged at the corner of the one on which he was resting.

This was intolerable!

He grabbed her by both shoulders and jerked her down on top of him and squashed his mouth against hers. He tried to force her lips open, at the same time pushing his hands down her back. All at once he felt a terrific blow on the side of his head. It stunned him. Green light flashed in his eyes and there was a sickening spasm in his stomach. He leaned over the edge of the sofa and that bicarbonate of soda he had had at the drugstore spilled into the inadequate cup of his hands.

He wiped them stupidly on his handkerchief.

"What did you hit me with?"

It was an unnecessary question. On the floor were shattered bits of blue pottery which he remembered seeing in the shape of a vase that contained a pair of sunflowers.

"You might have killed me with that," he said to her sadly.

She was standing over him, panting, and the disgust on her face was completely unfeigned.

"You make me sick!" she said. "Now please get out!"

THE room had not changed in his absence, only the light shone through a different window. The light was different. While he was gone upon his unhappy excursion about the city, the light in the room had performed the circuit of a lifetime, from violence to exhaustion. Now it did not stare at him nor make any harsh demands. It stayed near the window in a golden blur. The horsefly had also moved to that other window and showed a recession of power. Against the exterior light its delicate wings still glinted as points of blue flame, but the furious dives at the screen were now interspersed with periods of reflection which seemed to admit that failure was not any longer the least imaginable of all eventualities. Donald crossed immediately to the screen and gently unlatched it to let the fly out. He did this rather silly thing unconsciously, just as he opened doors for cats or children. He was a very kind man. There was something soft and passive about his mind which made it unusually responsive to the problems of creatures smaller or even weaker than himself. He stood awhile at the window. What was it this moment was trying to make him remember? Oh, my God, yes, that long-ago play he was in. That was his first acting job; he played the part of an adolescent coal miner who was killed in the collapse of a shaft. His mother was played by that old bitch Florence Kerwin. At the last curtain she slowly advanced to a window flooded with yellow gelatine and said in a tremulous whisper, "All sunsets are remembrance." There was a count of five and a very slow curtain. Before the curtain was down the seats were banging up and the little patter of applause was drowned in the shuffle of feet. The mysterious little Alabama spinster who wrote the play was standing breathlessly beside him in the wings as old Florence Kerwin came off.

The actress glared at them both and shouted. "The play's a turkey!"

The manager was standing there, too, and the spinster author turned to him uncomprehendingly.

"What is a turkey?" she asked.

"A bird with feathers!" he told her.

Donald had put his arm about her shoulders as she began to cry those tears that innocence is bathed in when it blunders trustfully into the glittering microcosm of Broadway, and over the quivering shoulders of Miss Charlotte Something or Other, who never was heard of again, he could see the coldly furious little manager tacking the closing notice upon the board.

Now Donald began to look around for the note Rachel must have left to explain her very long absence. He looked everywhere that a note might conceivably be left, even under the bed and the stove in case it had blown to the floor. At last he opened the closet where Rachel kept her clothes. Then for the second time that afternoon he received a blow that all but cracked his skull. Her clothes were gone from the closet. Her suitcase was also gone. Almost nothing remained but empty hangers.

Rachel is not coming back!

Until his blurred sight focused he moved toward the wall where against her protests he kept the picture of Rachel as a Glow Worm. On her lips was the gay, artificial smile of show business, the spangled tutu was lifted to show her bare thighs. Her bosom was visible through the sheer band of chiffon, no one had ever had such a lovely bosom as Rachel still had, but then . . .

In just a few moments the curtain of the finale would be coming down and they would go out to eat and then home to bed. In the hotel room a shade would be lowered for the beginning of something instead of the end. Oh, God, what pleasure those early nights had contained, things that couldn't even be said with music! Wasn't it natural to be vain in those days? It wasn't ridiculous to be vain in those days, both of them young and both of them lovely, then, coming together with such a crazed abandon that daylight would crowd the windows before their hands and arms and mouths would begin to let go of each other. Then they would go out to breakfast without having slept, no stockings on Rachel, he without socks or tie, and gorge themselves, hungry as wolves, on bowls of steaming cereal and cups of sweet black coffee and platters of bacon and eggs. What did they say to each other? It didn't seem that they ever talked to each other; he couldn't remember conversations between them. It was all longing and satisfaction of longing. They helped each other undress when they had returned from breakfast, gently each took the other's shoes off, and they fell on the bed like a pair of rag dolls a child dropped there, their bodies athwart each other in silly positions, so much light in the room for people to sleep in but not enough to keep them awake much longer . . .

Oh, Rachel, where have you gone?

No other refuge was thinkable but sleep, so he went to the bed and lifelessly took off his clothes. Under the covers he doubled his body up in the round, embryonic position. He closed his teeth on a corner of the pillow, the one that was hers, and began to release his tears.

Rachel, Rachel! Oh, Rachel!

Then all at once he heard her returning footsteps.

All in a rush of calling and sobbing she entered. Before he could lift his shoulders from the bed she had fallen upon him. She tore back the covers and scalded his face with her tears. Her cheekbones were awfully sharp. There was so little flesh on her arms, they were actually skinny, and yet they embraced him so fiercely he couldn't breathe.

"Oh, Rachel," he sobbed, and she moaned, "Donald, Donald!"

The name of a person you love is more than language — but after a while, when their sobbing had quieted a little, he held her fiery head in the crook of his arm and began to recite the litany of his sorrows. He told her about his misfortunes, the ones of this day and the probable ones of tomorrow. He told her about his illness, his palpitations, his possible death before long. He told her his beauty was lost, his time was now past. He had not been given that part he had counted upon. Strangers had laughed at him on the street. And Jane had misunderstood him; she had struck him over the head with a piece of blue pottery that might have killed him —

And Rachel whose sorrows were scarcely less than his own, said nothing about them but set her lips on his throat and answered with infinite softness to everything that he told her, "I know, I know!"

THE MYSTERIES OF
THE JOY RIO

The MYSTERIES
OF THE JOY RIO

Perhaps because he was a watch repairman, Mr. Gonzales had grown to be rather indifferent to time. A single watch or clock can be a powerful influence on a man, but when a man lives among as many watches and clocks as crowded the tiny, dim shop of Mr. Gonzales, some lagging behind, some skipping ahead, but all ticking monotonously on in their witless fashion, the multitude of them may be likely to deprive them of importance, as a gem loses its value when there are too many just like it which are too easily or cheaply obtainable. At any rate, Mr. Gonzales kept very irregular hours, if he could be said to keep any hours at all, and if he had not been where he was for such a long time, his trade would have suffered badly. But Mr. Gonzales had occupied his tiny shop for more than twenty years, since he had come to the city as a boy of nineteen to work as an apprentice to the original owner of the shop, a very strange and fat man of German descent named Kroger, Emiel Kroger, who had now been dead a long time. Emiel Kroger, being a romantically practical Teuton, had taken time, the commodity he worked with, with intense seriousness. In practically all his behavior he had imitated a perfectly adjusted fat silver watch. Mr. Gonzales, who was then young enough to be known as Pablo, had been his only sustained flirtation with the confusing, quicksilver world that exists outside of regularities. He had met Pablo during a watchmakers' convention in Dallas, Texas, where Pablo, who had illegally come into the country from Mexico a few days before, was drifting hungrily about the streets, and at that time Mr. Gonzales, Pablo, had not grown plump but had a lustrous dark grace which had completely bewitched Mr. Kroger. For as I have noted already, Mr. Kroger was a fat and strange man, subject to the kind of bewitchment that the graceful young Pablo could cast. The spell was so strong that it interrupted the fleeting and furtive practices of a lifetime in Mr. Kroger and induced him to take the boy home with him, to his shop-residence, where Pablo, now grown to the mature and fleshy proportions of Mr. Gonzales, had lived ever since, for three years before the death of his protector and for more than seventeen years after that, as the inheritor of shop-residence, clocks, watches, and everything else that Mr. Kroger had owned except a few pieces of dining-room silver which Emiel Kroger had left as a token bequest to a married sister in Toledo.

Some of these facts are of dubious pertinence to the little history which is to be unfolded. The important one is the fact that Mr. Gonzales had managed to drift enviably apart from the regularities that rule most other lives. Some days he would not open his shop at all and some days he would open it only for an hour or two in the morning, or in the late evening when other shops had closed, and in spite of these caprices he managed to continue to get along fairly well, due to the excellence of his work, when he did it, the fact that he was so well established in his own quiet way, the advantage of his location in a neighborhood where nearly everybody had an old alarm-clock which had to be kept in condition to order their lives, (this community being one inhabited mostly by people with small-paying jobs), but it was also due in measurable part to the fact that the thrifty Mr. Kroger, when he finally succumbed to a chronic disease of the bowels, had left a tidy sum in government bonds, and this capital, bringing in about a hundred and seventy dollars a month, would have kept Mr. Gonzales going along in a commonplace but comfortable fashion even if he had declined to do anything whatsoever. It was a pity that the late, or rather long-ago, Mr. Kroger, had not understood what a fundamentally peaceable sort of young man he had taken under his wing. Too bad he couldn't have guessed how perfectly everything suited Pablo Gonzales. But youth does not betray its true nature as palpably as the later years do, and Mr. Kroger had taken the animated allure of his young protégé, the flickering lights in his eyes and his quick, nervous movements, his very grace and slimness, as meaning something difficult to keep hold of. And as the old gentleman declined in health, as he did quite steadily during the three years that Pablo lived with him, he was never certain that the incalculably precious bird flown into his nest was not one of sudden passage but rather the kind that prefers to keep a faithful commitment to a single place, the nest-building kind, and not only that, but the very-rare-indeed-kind that gives love back as generously as he takes it. The long-ago Mr. Kroger had paid little attention to his illness, even when it entered the stage of acute pain, so intense was his absorption in what he thought was the tricky business of holding Pablo close to him. If only he had known that for all this time after his decease the boy would still be in the watchshop, how it might have relieved him! But on the other hand, maybe this anxiety, mixed as it was with so much tenderness and sad delight, was actually a blessing, standing as it did between the dying old man and a concern with death.

Pablo had never flown. But the sweet bird of youth had flown from Pablo Gonzales, leaving him rather sad, with a soft yellow face that was just as round as the moon. Clocks and watches he fixed with marvelous delicacy and precision, but he paid no attention to them; he had grown as obliviously accustomed to their many small noises as someone grows to the sound of waves who has always lived by the sea. Although he wasn't aware of it, it was actually light by which he told time, and always in the afternoons when the light had begun to fail (through the narrow window and narrower, dusty skylight at the back of the shop), Mr. Gonzales automatically rose from his stooped position over littered table and gooseneck lamp, took off his close-seeing glasses with magnifying lenses, and took to the street. He did not go far and he always went in the same direction, across town toward the river where there was an old opera house, now converted into a third-rate cinema, which specialized in the showing of cowboy pictures and other films of the sort that have a special appeal to children and male adolescents. The name of this moviehouse was the Joy Rio, a name peculiar enough but nowhere nearly so peculiar as the place itself.

The old opera house was a miniature of all the great opera houses of the old world, which is to say its interior was faded gilt and incredibly old and abused red damask which extended upwards through at least three tiers and possibly five. The upper stairs, that is, the stairs beyond the first gallery, were roped off and unlighted and the top of the theater was so peculiarly dusky, even with the silver screen flickering far below it, that Mr. Gonzales, used as he was to close work, could not have made it out from below. Once he had been there when the lights came on in the Joy Rio, but the coming on of the lights had so enormously confused and embarrassed him, that looking up was the last thing in the world he felt like doing. He had buried his nose in the collar of his coat and had scuttled out as quickly as a cockroach makes for the nearest shadow when a kitchen light comes on.

I have already suggested that there was something a bit special and obscure about Mr. Gonzales' habitual attendance at the Joy Rio, and that was my intention. For Mr. Gonzales had inherited more than the material possessions of his dead benefactor: he had also come into custody of his old protector's fleeting and furtive practices in dark places, the practices which Emiel Kroger had given up only when Pablo had come into his fading existence. The old man had left Mr. Gonzales the full gift of his shame, and now Mr. Gonzales did the sad, lonely things that Mr. Kroger had done for such a long time before his one lasting love came to him. Mr. Kroger had even practiced those things in the same place in which they were practiced now by Mr. Gonzales, in the many mysterious recesses of the Joy Rio, and Mr. Gonzales knew about this. He knew about it because Mr. Kroger had told him. Emiel Kroger had confessed his whole life and soul to Pablo Gonzales. It was his theory, the theory of most immoralists, that the soul becomes intolerably burdened with lies that have to be told to the world in order to be permitted to live in the world, and that unless this burden is relieved by entire honesty with *some one* person, who is trusted and adored, the soul will finally collapse beneath its weight of falsity. Much of the final months of the life of Emiel Kroger, increasingly dimmed by morphia, were devoted to these whispered confessions to his adored apprentice, and it was as if he had breathed the guilty soul of his past into the ears and brain and blood of the youth who listened, and not long after the death of Mr. Kroger, Pablo, who had stayed slim until then, had begun to accumulate fat. He never became anywhere nearly so gross as Emiel Kroger had been, but his delicate frame disappeared sadly from view among the irrelevant curves of a sallow plumpness. One by one the perfections which he had owned were folded away as Pablo put on fat as a widow puts on black garments. For a year beauty lingered about him, ghostly, continually fading, and then it went out altogether, and at twenty-five he was already the nondescriptly plump and moonfaced little man that he now was at forty, and if in his waking hours somebody to whom he would have to give a true answer had enquired of him, Pablo Gonzales, how much do you think about the dead Mr. Kroger, he probably would have shrugged and said, *Not much now. It's such a long time ago.* But if the question were asked him while he slept, the guileless heart of the sleeper would have responded, *Always, always!*

II

Now across the great marble stairs, that rose above the first gallery of the Joy Rio to the uncertain number of galleries above it, there had been fastened a greasy and rotting length of old velvet rope at the center of which was hung a sign that said to *Keep Out.* But that rope had not always been there. It had been there about twenty years, but the late Mr. Kroger had known the Joy Rio in the days before the flight of stairs was roped off. In those days the mysterious upper galleries of the Joy Rio had been a sort of fiddler's green where practically every device and fashion of carnality had run riot in a gloom so thick that a chance partner could only be discovered by touch. There were not rows of benches (as there were now on the orchestra level and the one gallery still kept in use), but strings of tiny boxes, extending in semicircles from one side of the great proscenium to the other. In some of these boxes broken-legged chairs might be found lying on their sides and shreds of old hangings still clung to the sliding brass loops at the entrances. According to Emiel Kroger, who is our only authority on these mysteries which share his remoteness in time, one lived up there, in the upper reaches of the Joy Rio, an almost sightless existence where the other senses, the senses of smell and touch and hearing, had to develop a preternatural keenness in order to spare one from making awkward mistakes, such as taking hold of the knee of a boy when it was a girl's knee one looked for, and where sometimes little scenes of panic occurred when a mistake of gender or of compatibility had been carried to a point where radical correction was called for. There had been many fights, there had even been rape and murder in those ancient boxes, till finally the obscure management of the Joy Rio had been compelled by the pressure of notoriety to shut down that part of the immense old building which had offered its principal enticement, and the Joy Rio, which had flourished until then, had then gone into sharp decline. It had been closed down and then reopened and closed down and reopened again. For several years it had opened and shut like a nervous lady's fan. Those were the years in which Mr. Kroger was dying. After his death the fitful era subsided, and now for about ten years the Joy Rio had been continually active as a third-rate cinema, closed only for one week during a threatened epidemic of poliomyelitis some years past and once for a few days when a small fire had damaged the projection booth. But nothing happened there now of a nature to provoke a disturbance. There were no complaints to the management or the police, and the dark glory of the upper galleries was a legend in such memories as that of the late Emiel Kroger and the present Pablo Gonzales, and one by one, of course, those memories died out and the legend died out with them. Places like the Joy Rio and the legends about them make one more than usually aware of the short bloom and the long fading out of things. The angel of such a place is a fat silver angel of sixty-three years in a shiny dark-blue alpaca jacket, with short, fat fingers that leave a damp mark where they touch, that sweat and tremble as they caress between whispers, an angel of such a kind as would be kicked out of heaven and laughed out of hell and admitted to earth only by grace of its habitual slyness, its gift for making itself a counterfeit being, and the connivance of those that a quarter tip and an old yellow smile can corrupt.

But the reformation of the Joy Rio was somewhat less than absolute. It had reformed only to the point of ostensible virtue, and in the back rows of the first gallery at certain hours in the afternoon and very late at night were things going on of the sort Mr. Gonzales sometimes looked for. At those hours the Joy Rio contained few patrons, and since the seats in the orchestra were in far better condition, those who had come to sit comfortably watching the picture would naturally remain downstairs; the few that elected to sit in the nearly deserted rows of the first gallery did so either because smoking was permitted in that section — or *because* . . .

There was a danger, of course, there always is a danger with places and things like that, but Mr. Gonzales was a tentative person not given to leaping before he looked. If a patron had entered the first gallery only in order to smoke, you could usually count on his occupying a seat along the aisle. If the patron had bothered to edge his way toward the center of a row of seats irregular as the jawbone of poor Yorick, one could assume as infallibly as one can assume anything in a universe where chance is the one invariable, that he had chosen his seat with something more than a cigarette in mind. Mr. Gonzales did not take many chances. This was a respect in which he paid due homage to the wise old spirit of the late Emiel Kroger, that romantically practical Teuton who used to murmur to Pablo, between sleeping and waking, a sort of incantation that went like this: Sometimes you will find it and other times you won't find it and the times you don't find it are the times when you have got to be careful. Those are the times when you have got to remember that other times you *will* find it, not *this* time but the *next* time, or the time *after* that, and then you've got to be able to go home without it, yes, those times are the times when you have got to be able to go home without it, go home *alone* without it . . .

Pablo didn't know, then, that he would ever have need of this practical wisdom that his benefactor had drawn from his almost lifelong pursuit of a pleasure which was almost as unreal and basically unsatisfactory as an embrace in a dream. Pablo didn't know then that he would inherit so much from the old man who took care of him, and at that time, when Emiel Kroger, in the dimness of morphia and weakness following hemorrhage, had poured into the delicate ear of his apprentice, drop by slow, liquid drop, this distillation of all he had learned in the years before he found Pablo, the boy had felt for this whisper the same horror and pity that he felt for the mortal disease in the flesh of his benefactor, and only gradually, in the long years since the man and his whisper had ceased, had the singsong rigmarole begun to have sense for him, a practical wisdom that such a man as Pablo had turned into, a man such as Mr. Gonzales, could live by safely and quietly and still find pleasure . . .

III

MR. GONZALES was careful, and for careful people life has a tendency to take on the character of an almost arid plain with only here and there, at wide intervals, the solitary palm tree and its shadow and the spring alongside it. Mr. Kroger's life had been much the same until he had come across Pablo at the watchmakers' convention in Dallas. But so far in Mr. Gonzales' life there had been no Pablo. In his life there had been only Mr. Kroger and the sort of things that Mr. Kroger had looked for and sometimes found but most times continued patiently to look for in the great expanse of arid country which his lifetime had been before the discovery of Pablo. And since it is not my intention to spin this story out any longer than its content seems to call for, I am not going to attempt to sustain your interest in it with a descripion of the few palm trees on the uneventful desert through which the successor to Emiel Kroger wandered after the death of the man who had been his

213

life. But I am going to remove you rather precipitately to a summer afternoon which we will call *Now* when Mr. Gonzales learned that he was dying, and not only dying but dying of the same trouble that had put the period under the question mark of Emiel Kroger. The scene, if I can call it that, takes place in a doctor's office. After some hedging on the part of the doctor, the word malignant is uttered. The hand is placed on the shoulder, almost contemptuously comforting, and Mr. Gonzales is assured that surgery is unnecessary because the condition is not susceptible to any help but that of drugs to relax the afflicted organs. And after that the scene is abruptly blacked out . . .

Now it is a year later. Mr. Gonzales has recovered more or less from the shocking information that he received from his doctor. He has been repairing watches and clocks almost as well as ever, and there has been remarkably little alteration in his way of life. Only a little more frequently is the shop closed. It is apparent, now, that the disease from which he suffers does not intend to destroy him any more suddenly than it destroyed the man before him. It grows slowly, the growth, and in fact it has recently shown signs of what is called a remission. There is no pain, hardly any and hardly ever. The most palpable symptom is loss of appetite and, as a result of that, a steady decrease of weight. Now rather startlingly, after all this time, the graceful approximation of Pablo's delicate structure has come back out of the irrelevant contours which had engulfed it after the long-ago death of Emiel Kroger. The mirrors are not very good in the dim little residence-shop, where he lives in his long wait for death, and when he looks in them, Mr. Gonzales sees the boy that was loved by the man whom he loved. It is almost Pablo. Pablo has almost returned from Mr. Gonzales.

And then one afternoon . . .

IV

THE new usher at the Joy Rio was a boy of seventeen and the little Jewish manager had told him that he must pay particular attention to the roped-off staircase to see to it that nobody slipped upstairs to the forbidden region of the upper galleries, but this boy was in love with a girl named Gladys who came to the Joy Rio every afternoon, now that school was let out for the summer, and loitered around the entrance where George, the usher, was stationed. She wore a thin, almost transparent, white blouse with nothing much underneath it. Her skirt was usually of sheer silken material that followed her heart-shaped loins as raptly as George's hand followed them when he embraced her in the dark ladies' room on the balcony level of the Joy Rio. Sensual delirium possessed him those afternoons when Gladys loitered near him. But the recently changed management of the Joy Rio was not a strict one, and in the summer vigilance was more than commonly relaxed. George stayed near the downstairs entrance, twitching restively in his tight, faded uniform till Gladys drifted in from the afternoon streets on a slow tide of lilac perfume. She would seem not to see him as she sauntered up the aisle he indicated with his flashlight and took a seat in the back of the orchestra section where he could find her easily when the "coast

215

was clear," or if he kept her waiting too long and she was more than usually bored with the film, she would stroll back out to the lobby and inquire in her childish drawl, Where is the Ladies' Room, Please? Sometimes he would curse her fiercely under his breath because she hadn't waited. But he would have to direct her to the staircase, and she would go up there and wait for him, and the knowledge that she was up there waiting would finally overpower his prudence to the point where he would even abandon his station if the little manager, Mr. Katz, had his office door wide open. The ladies' room was otherwise not in use. Its light-switch was broken, or if it was repaired, the bulbs would be mysteriously missing. When ladies other than Gladys enquired about it, George would say gruffly, The ladies' room's out of order. It made an almost perfect retreat for the young lovers. The door left ajar gave warning of footsteps on the grand marble staircase in time for George to come out with his hands in his pockets before whoever was coming could catch him at it. But these interruptions would sometimes infuriate him, especially when a patron would insist on borrowing his flashlight to use the cabinet in the room where Gladys waited with her crumpled silk skirt gathered high about her flanks (leaning against the invisible dried-up washbasin) which were the blazing black heart of the insatiably concave summer.

In the old days Mr. Gonzales used to go to the Joy Rio in the late afternoons but since his illness he had been going earlier because the days tired him earlier, especially the steaming days of August which were now in

216

progress. Mr. Gonzales knew about George and Gladys; he made it his business, of course, to know everything there was to be known about the Joy Rio, which was his earthly heaven, and, of course, George also knew about Mr. Gonzales; he knew why Mr. Gonzales gave him a fifty cent tip every time he inquired his way to the men's room upstairs, each time as if he had never gone upstairs before. Sometimes George muttered something under his breath, but the tributes collected from patrons like Mr. Gonzales had so far ensured his complicity in their venal practices. But then one day in August, on one of the very hottest and blindingly bright afternoons, George was so absorbed in the delights of Gladys that Mr. Gonzales had arrived at the top of the stairs to the balcony before George heard his footsteps. Then he heard them and he clamped a sweating palm over the mouth of Gladys which was full of stammerings of his name and the name of God. He waited, but Mr. Gonzales also waited. Mr. Gonzales was actually waiting at the top of the stairs to recover his breath from the climb, but George, who could see him, now, through the door kept slightly ajar, suspected that he was waiting to catch him coming out of his secret place. A fury burst in the boy. He thrust Gladys violently back against the washbasin and charged out of the room without even bothering to button his fly. He rushed up to the slight figure waiting near the stairs and began to shout a dreadful word at Mr. Gonzales, the word "morphodite." His voice was shrill as a jungle bird's, shouting this word "morphodite." Mr. Gonzales kept backing away from him, with the lightness and grace of his youth, he kept stepping backwards from the livid face and threatening fists of the usher, all the time murmuring, No, no, no, no, no. The youth stood between him and the stairs below so it was toward the upper staircase that Mr. Gonzales took flight. All at once, as quickly and lightly as ever Pablo had moved, he darted under the length of velvet rope with the sign "Keep Out." George's pursuit was interrupted by the manager of the theater, who seized his arm so fiercely that the shoulder-seam of the uniform burst apart. This started another disturbance under the cover of which Mr. Gonzales fled farther and farther up the forbidden staircase into regions of deepening shadow. There were several points at which he might safely have stopped but his flight had now gathered an irresistible momentum and his legs moved like pistons bearing him up and up, and then ——

At the very top of the staircase he was intercepted. He half turned back when he saw the dim figure waiting above, he almost turned and scrambled back down the grand marble staircase, when the name of his youth was called to him in a tone so commanding that he stopped and waited without daring to look up again.

Pablo, said Mr. Kroger, come on up here, Pablo.

Mr. Gonzales obeyed, but now the false power that his terror had given him was drained out of his body and he climbed with effort. At the top of the stairs where Emiel Kroger waited, he would have sunk exhausted to his knees if the old man hadn't sustained him with a firm hand at his elbow.

Mr. Kroger said, This way, Pablo. He led him into the Stygian blackness of one of the little boxes in the

218

once-golden horseshoe of the topmost tier. Now sit down, he commanded.

Pablo was too breathless to say anything except, Yes, and Mr. Kroger leaned over him and unbuttoned his collar for him, unfastened the clasp of his belt, all the while murmuring, There now, there now, Pablo.

The panic disappeared under those soothing old fingers and the breathing slowed down and stopped hurting the chest as if a fox was caught in it, and then at last Mr. Kroger began to lecture the boy as he used to, Pablo, he murmured, don't ever be so afraid of being lonely that you forget to be careful. Don't forget that you will find it sometimes but other times you won't be lucky, and those are the times when you have got to be patient, since patience is what you must have when you don't have luck.

The lecture continued softly, reassuringly familiar and repetitive as the tick of a bedroom clock in his ear, and if his ancient protector and instructor, Emiel Kroger, had not kept all the while soothing him with the moist, hot touch of his tremulous fingers, the gradual, the very gradual dimming out of things, his fading out of existence, would have terrified Pablo. But the ancient voice and fingers, as if they had never left him, kept on unbuttoning, touching, soothing, repeating the ancient lesson, saying it over and over like a penitent counting prayer beads, Sometimes you will have it and sometimes you won't have it, so don't be anxious about it. You must always be able to go home alone without it. Those are the times when you have got to remember that other times you will have it and it doesn't matter if sometimes you don't have it and have to go home without it, go home alone without it, go home alone without it. The gentle advice went on, and as it went on, Mr. Gonzales drifted away from everything but the wise old voice in his ear, even at last from that, but not till he was entirely comforted by it.

New Directions Paperbooks

Walter Abish, *Alphabetical Africa*. NDP375.
 In the Future Perfect. NDP440.
 Minds Meet. NDP387.
Ilangô Adigal, *Shilappadikaram*. NDP162.
Alain, *The Gods*. NDP382.
David Antin. *Talking at the Boundaries*. NDP388.
G. Apollinaire, *Selected Writings*.† NDP310.
Djuna Barnes, *Nightwood*. NDP98.
Charles Baudelaire, *Flowers of Evil*.† NDP71.
 Paris Spleen. NDP294.
Martin Bax. *The Hospital Ship*. NDP402.
Gottfried Benn, *Primal Vision*.† NDP322.
Jorge Luis Borges, *Labyrinths*. NDP186.
Jean-François Bory, *Once Again*. NDP256.
Kay Boyle, *Thirty Stores*. NDP62.
E. Brock, *The Blocked Heart*. NDP399.
 Here. Now. Always. NDP429.
 Invisibility Is The Art of Survival. NDP342.
 Paroxisms. NDP385.
 The Portraits & The Poses. NDP360.
Buddha, *The Dhammapada*. NDP188.
Frederick Busch, *Domestic Particulars*. NDP413.
 Manual Labor. NDP376.
Ernesto Cardenal, *Apocalypse & Other Poems*. NDP441.
 In Cuba. NDP377.
Hayden Carruth, *For You*. NDP298.
 From Snow and Rock, from Chaos. NDP349.
Louis-Ferdinand Céline,
 Death on the Installment Plan. NDP330.
 Guignol's Band. NDP278.
 Journey to the End of the Night. NDP84.
Stephen Clissold, *The Wisdom of the Spanish Mystics*. NDP442.
Jean Cocteau, *The Holy Terrors*. NDP212.
 The Infernal Machine. NDP235.
M. Cohen, *Monday Rhetoric*. NDP352.
Cid Corman, *Livingdying*. NDP289.
 Sun Rock Man. NDP318.
Gregory Corso, *Elegiac Feelings American*. NDP299.
 Happy Birthday of Death. NDP86.
 Long Live Man. NDP127.
Kenneth Cragg, *Wisdom of the Sufis*. NDP424.
Edward Dahlberg, *Reader*. NDP246.
 Because I Was Flesh. NDP227.
David Daiches, *Virginia Woolf*. NDP96.
Osamu Dazai, *The Setting Sun*. NDP258.
 No Longer Human. NDP357.
Coleman Dowell, *Mrs. October . . . NDP368.
Robert Duncan, *Bending the Bow*. NDP255.
 The Opening of the Field. NDP356.
 Roots and Branches. NDP275.
Richard Eberhart, *Selected Poems*. NDP198.
Russell Edson. *The Falling Sickness*. NDP 389.
 The Very Thing That Happens. NDP137.
Paul Eluard, *Uninterrupted Poetry*. NDP392.
Wm. Empson, *7 Types of Ambiguity*. NDP204.
 Some Versions of Pastoral. NDP92.
Wm. Everson, *Man-Fate*. NDP369.
 The Residual Years. NDP263.
Lawrence Ferlinghetti, *Her*. NDP88.
 Back Roads to Far Places. NDP312.
 A Coney Island of the Mind. NDP74.
 The Mexican Night. NDP300.
 Open Eye, Open Heart. NDP361.
 Routines. NDP187.
 The Secret Meaning of Things. NDP268.
 Starting from San Francisco. NDP 220.
 Tyrannus Nix?. NDP288.
 Who Are We Now? NDP425.
Ronald Firbank, *Two Novels*. NDP128.
Dudley Fitts,
 Poems from the Greek Anthology. NDP60.
F. Scott Fitzgerald, *The Crack-up*. NDP54.
Robert Fitzgerald, *Spring Shade*. NDP311.
Gustave Flaubert,
 The Dictionary of Accepted Ideas. NDP230.
M. K. Gandhi, *Gandhi on Non-Violence*. (ed. Thomas Merton) NDP197.
André Gide, *Dostoevsky*. NDP100.
Goethe, *Faust*, Part I. (MacIntyre translation) NDP70.
Albert J. Guerard, *Thomas Hardy*. NDP185.

Henry Hatfield, *Goethe*. NDP136.
John Hawkes, *The Beetle Leg*. NDP239.
 The Blood Oranges. NDP338.
 The Cannibal. NDP123.
 Death, Sleep & The Traveler. NDP393.
 The Innocent Party. NDP238.
 John Hawkes Symposium. NDP446.
 The Lime Twig. NDP95.
 Lunar Landscapes. NDP274.
 The Owl. NDP443.
 Second Skin. NDP146.
 Travesty. NDP430.
A. Hayes, *A Wreath of Christmas Poems*. NDP347.
H.D., *Helen in Egypt*. NDP380
 Hermetic Definition NDP343.
 Trilogy. NDP362.
Robert E. Helbling, *Heinrich von Kleist*, NDP390.
Hermann Hesse, *Siddhartha*. NDP65.
C. Isherwood, *The Berlin Stories*. NDP134.
 Lions and Shadows. NDP435.
Philippe Jaccottet, *Seedtime*. NDP428.
Gustav Janouch,
 Conversations With Kafka. NDP313.
Alfred Jarry, *The Supermale*. NDP426.
 Ubu Roi, NDP105.
Robinson Jeffers, *Cawdor and Medea*. NDP293.
James Joyce, *Stephen Hero*. NDP133.
 James Joyce/Finnegans Wake. NDP331.
Franz Kafka, *Amerika*. NDP117.
Bob Kaufman,
 Solitudes Crowded with Loneliness. NDP199.
Hugh Kenner, *Wyndham Lewis*. NDP167.
Kenyon Critics, *Gerard Manley Hopkins*. NDP355.
P. Lal, *Great Sanskrit Plays*. NDP142.
Tommaso Landolfi,
 Gogol's Wife and Other Stories. NDP155.
Lautréamont, *Maldoror*. NDP207.
Irving Layton, *Selected Poems*. NDP431.
Denise Levertov, *Footprints*. NDP344.
 The Freeing of the Dust. NDP401.
 The Jacob's Ladder. NDP112.
 O Taste and See. NDP149.
 The Poet in the World. NDP363.
 Relearning the Alphabet. NDP290.
 The Sorrow Dance. NDP222.
 To Stay Alive. NDP325.
 With Eyes at the Back of Our Heads. NDP229.
Harry Levin, *James Joyce*. NDP87.
Garcia Lorca, *Five Plays*. NDP232.
 Selected Poems.† NDP114.
 Three Tragedies. NDP52.
Michael McClure, *Gorf*. NDP416.
 Jaguar Skies. NDP400.
 September Blackberries. NDP370.
Carson McCullers, *The Member of the Wedding*. (Playscript) NDP153.
Thomas Merton, *Asian Journal*. NDP394.
 Gandhi on Non-Violence. NDP197.
 The Geography of Lograire. NDP283.
 My Argument with the Gestapo. NDP403.
 New Seeds of Contemplation. NDP337.
 Raids on the Unspeakable. NDP213.
 Selected Poems. NDP85.
 The Way of Chuang Tzu. NDP276.
 The Wisdom of the Desert. NDP295.
 Zen and the Birds of Appetite. NDP261.
Henri Michaux, *Selected Writings*.† NDP264.
Henry Miller, *The Air-Conditioned Nightmare*. NDP302.
 Big Sur & The Oranges of Hieronymus Bosch. NDP161.
 The Books in My Life. NDP280.
 The Colossus of Maroussi. NDP75.
 The Cosmological Eye. NDP109.
 Henry Miller on Writing. NDP151.
 The Henry Miller Reader. NDP269.
 Remember to Remember. NDP111.
 The Smile at the Foot of the Ladder. NDP386.
 Stand Still Like the Hummingbird. NDP236.
 The Time of the Assassins. NDP115.
 The Wisdom of the Heart. NDP94.
Y. Mishima, *Confessions of a Mask*. NDP253.
 Death in Midsummer. NDP215.

Eugenio Montale, *New Poems.* NDP410.
  Selected Poems.† NDP193.
Vladimir Nabokov, *Nikolai Gogol.* NDP78.
  The Real Life of Sebastian Knight. NDP432.
P. Neruda, *The Captain's Verses.*† NDP345.
  Residence on Earth.† NDP340.
New Directions in Prose & Poetry (Anthology).
  Available from #17 forward. #35, *Fall 1977.*
Robert Nichols, *Arrival.* NDP437.
Charles Olson, *Selected Writings.* NDP231.
Toby Olson. *The Life of Jesus.* NDP417.
George Oppen, *Collected Poems.* NDP418.
Wilfred Owen, *Collected Poems.* NDP210.
Nicanor Parra, *Emergency Poems.*† NDP333.
  Poems and Antipoems.† NDP242.
G. Parrinder, *Wisdom of the Early Buddhists.*
  NDP444.
  Wisdom of the Forest. NDP414.
Boris Pasternak, *Safe Conduct.* NDP77.
Kenneth Patchen, *Aflame and Afun of*
  Walking Faces. NDP292.
  Because It Is. NDP83.
  But Even So. NDP255.
  Collected Poems. NDP284.
  Doubleheader. NDP211.
  Hallelujah Anyway. NDP219.
  In Quest of Candlelighters. NDP334.
  The Journal of Albion Moonlight. NDP99.
  Memoirs of a Shy Pornographer. NDP205.
  Selected Poems. NDP160.
  Sleepers Awake. NDP286.
  Wonderings. NDP320.
Octavio Paz, *Configurations.*† NDP303.
  Eagle or Sun? NDP422.
  Early Poems.† NDP354.
Plays for a New Theater. (Anth.) NDP216.
J. A. Porter, *Eelgrass.* NDP438.
Ezra Pound, *ABC of Reading.* NDP89.
  Classic Noh Theatre of Japan. NDP79.
  Confucius. NDP285.
  Confucius to Cummings. (Anth.) NDP126.
  Gaudier-Brzeska. NDP372.
  Guide to Kulchur. NDP257.
  Literary Essays. NDP250.
  Love Poems of Ancient Egypt. NDP178.
  Pavannes and Divagations. NDP397.
  Pound/Joyce. NDP296.
  Selected Cantos. NDP304.
  Selected Letters 1907-1941. NDP317.
  Selected Poems. NDP66.
  Selected Prose 1909-1965. NDP396.
  The Spirit of Romance. NDP266.
  Translations.† (Enlarged Edition) NDP145.
Omar Pound, *Arabic & Persian Poems.* NDP305.
James Purdy, *Children Is All.* NDP327.
Raymond Queneau, *The Bark Tree.* NDP314.
  The Flight of Icarus. NDP358.
  The Sunday of Life. NDP433.
Mary de Rachewiltz, *Ezra Pound:*
  Father and Teacher. NDP405.
M. Randall, *Part of the Solution.* NDP350.
John Crowe Ransom, *Beating the Bushes.*
  NDP324.
Raja Rao, *Kanthapura.* NDP224.
Herbert Read, *The Green Child.* NDP208.
P. Reverdy, *Selected Poems.*† NDP346.
Kenneth Rexroth, *Assays.* NDP113.
  Beyond the Mountains. NDP384.
  Bird in the Bush. NDP80.
  Collected Longer Poems. NDP309.
  Collected Shorter Poems. NDP243.
  Love and the Turning Year. NDP308.
  New Poems. NDP383.
  One Hundred More Poems from the Japanese.
  NDP420.
  100 Poems from the Chinese. NDP192.
  100 Poems from the Japanese.† NDP147.
Rainer Maria Rilke, *Poems from*
  The Book of Hours. NDP408.
  Possibility of Being. NDP436.
Arthur Rimbaud, *Illuminations.*† NDP56.
  Season in Hell & Drunken Boat.† NDP97.
Edouard Roditi, *Delights of Turkey.* NDP445.

Selden Rodman, *Tongues of Fallen Angels.*
  NDP373.
Jerome Rothenberg, *Poems for the Game*
  of Silence. NDP406.
  Poland/1931. NDP379.
Saikaku Ihara, *The Life of an Amorous*
  Woman. NDP270.
St. John of the Cross, *Poems.*† NDP341.
Jean-Paul Sartre, *Baudelaire.* NDP233.
  Nausea. NDP82.
  The Wall (Intimacy). NDP272.
I. Schloegl, *Wisdow of the Zen Masters.* NDP415.
Delmore Schwartz, *Selected Poems.* NDP241.
Stevie Smith, *Selected Poems.* NDP159.
Gary Snyder, *The Back Country.* NDP249.
  Earth House Hold. NDP267.
  Regarding Wave. NDP306.
  Turtle Island. NDP381.
Gilbert Sorrentino, *Splendide-Hôtel.* NDP364.
Enid Starkie, *Arthur Rimbaud.* NDP254.
Stendhal, *Lucien Leuwen.*
  Book II: *The Telegraph.* NDP108.
Jules Supervielle, *Selected Writings.*† NDP209.
W. Sutton, *American Free Verse.* NDP351.
Nathaniel Tarn, *Lyrics . . . Bride of God.* NDP391.
Dylan Thomas, *Adventures in the Skin Trade.*
  NDP183.
  A Child's Christmas in Wales. NDP181.
  Collected Poems 1934-1952. NDP316.
  The Doctor and the Devils. NDP297.
  Portrait of the Artist as a Young Dog.
  NDP51.
  Quite Early One Morning. NDP90.
  Under Milk Wood. NDP73.
Lionel Trilling, *E. M. Forster.* NDP189.
Martin Turnell, *Art of French Fiction.* NDP251.
  Baudelaire. NDP336.
Alan Unterman. *The Wisdom of the Jewish*
  Mystics. NDP423.
Paul Valéry, *Selected Writings.*† NDP184.
P. Van Ostaijen, *Feasts of Fear & Agony.*
  NDP411.
Elio Vittorini, *A Vittorini Omnibus.* NDP366.
  Women of Messina. NDP365.
Linda W. Wagner. *Interviews with William*
  Carlos Williams. NDP421.
Vernon Watkins, *Selected Poems.* NDP221.
Nathanael West, *Miss Lonelyhearts &*
  Day of the Locust. NDP125.
G. F. Whicher, tr., *The Goliard Poets.*† NDP206.
J. Williams, *An Ear in Bartram's Tree.* NDP335.
Tennessee Williams, *Camino Real.* NDP301.
  Cat on a Hot Tin Roof. NDP398.
  Dragon Country. NDP287.
  Eight Mortal Ladies Possessed. NDP374.
  The Glass Menagerie. NDP218.
  Hard Candy. NDP225.
  In the Winter of Cities. NDP154.
  One Arm & Other Stories. NDP237.
  Out Cry. NDP367.
  The Roman Spring of Mrs. Stone. NDP271.
  Small Craft Warnings. NDP348.
  Sweet Bird of Youth. NDP409.
  27 Wagons Full of Cotton. NDP217.
William Carlos Williams,
  The Autobiography. NDP223.
  The Build-up. NDP259.
  Embodiment of Knowledge. NDP434.
  The Farmers' Daughters. NDP106.
  Imaginations. NDP329.
  In the American Grain. NDP53.
  In the Money. NDP240.
  Many Loves. NDP191.
  Paterson. Complete. NDP152.
  Pictures from Brueghel. NDP118.
  The Selected Essays. NDP273.
  Selected Poems. NDP131.
  A Voyage to Pagany. NDP307.
  White Mule. NDP226.
  W. C. Williams Reader. NDP282.
Yvor Winters, *E. A. Robinson.* NDP326.

Complete descriptive catalog available free on request from
New Directions, 333 Sixth Avenue, New York 10014.   † Bilingual